D1241094

A Time for Judas

OTHER BOOKS BY MORLEY CALLAGHAN:

Strange Fugitive (1928)
An Autumn Penitent (1929)
A Native Argosy (1929)
It's Never Over (1930)
Broken Journey (1932)
Such Is My Beloved (1934)
They Shall Inherit the Earth (1935)
Now That April's Here (1936)
More Joy In Heaven (1937)
The Varsity Story (1945)
Luke Baldwin's Vow (1949)
The Loved and the Lost (1951)
The Many Colored Coat (1960)
A Passion in Rome (1961)
That Summer in Paris (1963)
A Fine and Private Place (1975)
Close to the Sun Again (1977)

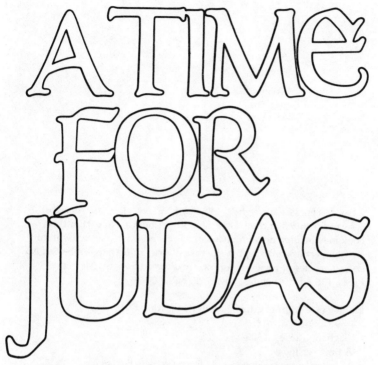

A TIME FOR JUDAS

BY Morley Callaghan

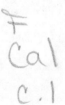

St. Martin's Press
New York

Library of Congress Cataloging in Publication Data

Callaghan, Morley, 1903-
  A time for Judas.
    1. Judas Iscariot—Fiction.   2. Jesus Christ—Fiction.
I. Title.
PR 9199.C27T55   1984   813'.52   84-2116
ISBN 0-312-80513-6

First Published in Canada by Macmillan of Canada

First U.S. Edition

10 9 8 7 6 5 4 3 2 1

Remembering Owen Spencer Davies

FOREWORD

Here is how I came upon Philo's story. Across the road from this television station was a bar where I often sat late in the afternoon, and I knew that at five o'clock a smooth man with thinning hair, wearing an expensive dark suit, would come hurrying in for a straight gin which he would gulp down; he would sit for a little while as if listening raptly to some enchanting, far-away wild music and then hurry out again. The bartender told me that his name was Owen Spencer Davies and he was a television producer.

One day Spencer Davies spoke to me. Two days later he wrote me a long letter about my work, which he seemed to know very well. The letter was full of insights, some of them downright embarrassing, and so charmed was I that I asked him to lunch with me. After that we had lunch once a week and I grew very fond of him. He told me he came from a monied old Welsh family, had spent a year at Cambridge, then had joined the Benedictine order and gone to Rome to study. Having a talent for Greek and Latin, he had found himself working in the Vatican library, where he had remained until he left the church. After he came to Canada everything had gone well for him until a year ago, when everything began to go wrong. The pretty young actress he had married died suddenly of pneumonia, and a month later he discovered that he had leukemia. Now he was taking chemotherapy treatments, was losing his hair, and was floating in gin.

Those dashes across the street from the television station to the bar finally did him in. When he was fired I began to see more of him. He had bald patches now. He was thinner, too. But there was another change in him; his eyes, turning inward, would shift around restlessly. Finally he told me he wanted to go to Rome and write a book, a job he had kept putting off; the long delay was driving him crazy and making him feel ashamed. He knew he could only do this book in Rome, he said, but he didn't have the money to go there. Owen's sense of desperate urgency, and the failing health that brought a wild glint in his eyes, began to depress me. Finally I loaned him five thousand dollars, which he was to repay me when a rich old uncle died, and off he went to Rome.

For months I didn't hear from him. Then around Christmas time I got a letter. He had good news, he said in the letter. He had had a remission of the leukemia. His health was good now. He was working furiously. His rich uncle, unfortunately, was still alive. The address he gave me was "Father Coutreau, the Canadian College at the Vatican." This father, I remembered, was the Québécois priest who had first talked to him about Canada.

The news of the remission so delighted me that I wrote saying that I had long planned to go to Rome to see my publisher and to meet my translator, and why shouldn't it be soon, so in no time we might be together again. I got a postcard in return asking when I was coming. What could I say? I was working on a book myself and it wasn't going well.

For a year I did not hear again from Owen Spencer Davies. Sometimes I wondered if he ever would be able to repay the loan. Then late in the fall, when I was thinking of the blue skies of Rome, I got a short letter from him. He wrote: "It has been set in my mind that you are coming here. Am I wrong? If you are coming make it soon — very soon. I must see you. I know I will, but please, come very soon." The plea in this letter upset me. I wrote to my translator, and to the Father Coutreau address; then within two weeks I set out for Rome.

Before noon I left the Excelsior and went along the Via

Veneto to the office of the publisher Montedori, where I learned that my translator had set out for Paris a week earlier. Disappointed, I got a taxi and headed for the Canadian College at the Vatican. A housekeeper took my name to Father Coutreau, who came to the door himself. A stocky, affable French Canadian, he asked me to have a cup of tea and some biscuits with him. For almost a year, he said, Owen had enjoyed the remission from the leukemia and had actually looked healthy. He had never told anyone what the book was about. A few months ago, unfortunately, the remission had ended, but Owen had gone on working, refusing to go to the hospital, and now was in bad shape. He was waiting to see me. When and where? I said that at five o'clock that afternoon I would be sitting at that café on the Piazza del Popolo, the one where you can sit and look up at the Pincio.

I was there, as I said I would be, and the soft bluish mist was touching all the hills of Rome. Within ten minutes a taxi pulled up almost in front of my table and a gaunt, thin man got out. I mightn't have known Owen if he hadn't smiled at me. In spite of his suffering, some serenity in that faint smile held me speechless. Shaken, wondering where I had seen that head before and that thin face with the haunting smile, I thought of the sculptured head in the Cathedral at Chartres held in the light of those glorious blue windows. After we had shaken hands he said, "Ah, these remissions. A sick man begins to believe he has won out. Now it has to be more of the damn chemotherapy." And while asking about people in my home town he kept smiling at me approvingly. That I was there at last seemed to be giving him immense satisfaction.

He had a Cinzano with me; then after a little small talk which only seemed to deepen his sense of urgency he told me the story of an Italian professor whom he had met and grown to love when he was working in the Vatican archives. This sixty-five-year-old professor was considered to be the best of all the Middle East archeologists and scholars of biblical times. He had a white pointed beard and a bald head and a limp in his left leg from a war wound, and was supposed to be cold and disdainful and aloof. "But I remember the day he got talking to me about Elizabethan love lyrics," Owen said, "and then invited me to dinner." At dinner Owen discovered that this apparently austere man had lost his son in a drowning and now was lonely, and dreamed of being in the company of a young man he could talk to as freely as he had once talked to his own son. He had eyes so shrewd and intelligent they could make you feel uncomfortable, but if he were suddenly pleased, the eyes would be full of warmth and laughter. One night he said, "I find it strange I talk to you as I would talk to my own son, and yet I've known you such a little while. What is this recognition?"

He said this about the time the manuscripts written by a certain Philo of Crete were brought to him for verification of their authenticity.

This happened just after the Turkish sweep into the island of Cyprus, when Greek Cypriots were driven out of a whole section of the island and many of their villages were levelled. Someone digging around one of the ruined villas unearthed a sealed jar. The Greek jar, elegant and slim, had figures inset around it, a maiden in happy flight from a youth reaching out for her. Inside were manuscripts. Whoever had found the jar knew how valuable the manuscripts were to the Vatican theologians. Who put up the money to acquire them was hard to say. Anyway, they were brought to the professor.

At one of their dinners, Owen said, he found the professor in a state of feverish excitement. The professor wouldn't tell what had happened, yet he acted like a stunned or dazzled young scholar. All he would say was that he had been asked for his opinion on the authenticity of certain manuscripts from the first century, and, oh, they were authentic all right! There was no question about their authenticity, and he had made his report to certain powerful churchmen.

Within a week, while the manuscripts were still in his possession, the professor had become another man, nervous and worried. One night he wanted Owen to come to his house, and at first it was like any other evening. But in the long silences he seemed to be reaching out for intimacy and trust. Finally tears came to his eyes. Well, Owen said, the tears running down his cheeks were simply shattering. It was plain he had to talk to someone who was young and close to him.

He had been advised, the professor said, that the Philo manuscripts were to be regarded as the work of Gnostics, those early heretics who had come up with such things as the Gospel according to Thomas, and a Gospel according to Mary. "Owen, you're much younger than I am," he kept saying, as if youth in someone offered him a hope, a possibility of a way out of his terrible distress and his tears. The battle was in his own heart, the battle between the great scholar and the good church soldier. The scholar, in spite of all his integrity, knew he was losing, and in his despair he sought a strange satisfaction; he hoped that someone much younger would take the story of Philo of Crete and carry it around in his heart. Though hidden in the heart, it would still be alive in this younger man.

"Well, that night I read all the writings," Owen said softly. "The manuscript was in good condition, and my Greek was good enough. I read and read and read again, and I made notes as I read. When I got home, that great old man's tears began to outrage me. I sat down and made more notes. Fresh from the reading, I made note after note as stuff came back to me. I sat up all night, living in Philo's meditations, and at dawn, exhausted on the bed, I wanted to know why it was enough for the professor to know that the story still lived in the mind of someone much younger.

"Well, within a week I learned why he had wept. The manuscripts were taken from him. Word had gone out that they were to be pronounced forgeries, and that in any event their age could not be authenticated. That was the word. So they were to be destroyed. And that great old man accepted this judgment. My God, he accepted it! What do you do with a great and fine old man who permits a thing to be done as the good right thing in the service of an institution which has been his whole life, when he knows that in acquiescing he'll be haunted and ashamed the rest of his life? Ashamed of doing the right thing."

Anyway, right away the professor had gone into complete retirement in a hill town in northern Italy. "As for me," Owen said, "I kept all the notes. Pages and pages of the notes. I put them away. Time passed, but I think Philo, always in the back of my mind, was nagging away at me and driving me crazy."

The high, unnatural color had vanished from his cheeks; they now had an awful gray shade as he leaned over the table. He said he had made a book out of the notes, a story, because Philo believed so much in legends and storytelling. It was everything to him. "I've written the story," he said. "I should have gone to the hospital three weeks ago, but I had to finish the whole story. I want to get it to you . . ." But the utter exhaustion so apparent in him after his sigh of relief frightened me. "Come on, Owen, I'll get you home," I said.

He lived in the Via Margutta, where so many painters lived. At the house he wouldn't let me help him climb the stairs. The young woman he lived with, a painter, would be waiting for him, he said, and I embraced him and we parted.

Entering my hotel around midnight, I saw an elegant tall girl in a leather jacket leaving the desk. The desk clerk, calling out to me, gave me a big manila envelope. I opened it there in the lobby — a manuscript entitled "According to Philo of Crete." There was also a note from Owen. He wrote, "My dear friend. About the language I've had Philo use! I feel I know him well, and I couldn't bear to try and have him sound stiff and archaic. So the language here is direct — as in natural speech — sometimes even verging on the colloquial." That was all.

Just before noon the next day Father Coutreau called to say that Owen had been taken to the hospital in a coma. He died in the hospital.

But here is the manuscript.

I

Not far from the Jerusalem wall are vineyards with grapes of a very special flavor, and that first time in Judea when I was the senator's agent buying wine and olives for shipment to Rome, I used to think the Jews were like these grapes. These hook-nosed people had their own flavor, their own spiritual isolation, their own barbaric splendor, and it fascinated me that they had been able to hold on to these things in spite of the Greek and Roman influences. Yet as I had soon learned when I was there as a merchant, nothing in Judea is as it appears to be. The story is in those Judean hills. In the springtime those hills have a beautiful lush greenness slashed with the purple of the valleys, and then, as the light changes, the purple slashes become golden bands, binding the hills in an enchanting peacefulness; yet those hills are filled with bandits, waiting to raid caravans, and men who would be kings, dreaming of swooping down on Jerusalem, and of course these patriotic kings are just bandits too. It was a wild time, my time as a merchant.

Since I had taken the trouble to learn the language, I had many Jewish friends and spent more time with them than with the Romans. Soon the pretty wife of a dull but politically ambitious priest told me she was lonely. She liked listening to me talk about Athens, Rome, and Egypt, even my home in Crete, saying wistfully that she kept seeing herself in those places with me. I liked undoing her waist-long shiny black hair, and when it fell around her naked shoulders, curling around her breasts, she had mystery for me — all of a woman's mystery in her hair.

But one afternoon on the bed when she was twining her hair around my neck, her husband came in. I had to run. I had never really trusted the rich discontented young widow who had introduced us. And the young priest brought a charge of adultery against his wife, and proved it. She was to be taken to the east gate, stripped to the waist, and left there, tied up, to be mocked and degraded by any passerby.

It was a terrible time for me. But before these things could be done, the young wife got a congestion on her chest and a high fever from those damp Jerusalem stone houses. I heard about these things from the physician, my friend Ezekiel. They had prepared her for death, he said. As her husband watched her dying, he began to weep and to pray. Again and again he went to the temple, wailing and praying, fasting, throwing himself on the floor, and, according to the physician, keeping her alive with his prayers and loving her as he had never done before. She lived and was forgiven, with everybody wondering and rejoicing at the triumph of prayers and love.

I felt thankful and safe till the night when I was

stabling my horse and a man came out of the shadows, moonlight suddenly on his thick neck and contorted face and glinting on his knife, too. When I slashed at him with my short sword, he screamed. Both hands to his head, he kept on screaming. Then, dropping his blood-stained hands, he stared at them, then at the ground, and with a wild frightened yell, he ran. The knife was at my feet near the bloody ear. Stooping, I stared at the ear. I knew the young priest would not be satisfied till I was killed.

Next day I ran for my life — back to Rome.

For two days I was afraid to face the senator. Finally I went to him and told what had happened. He was generous in his understanding. He knew about these things. "These Jewish women seem exotic to us in their sensuality, don't they?" he said. For a week he let me sit around in the villa. Then he gave me a promotion. He sent me to Alexandria to oversee the wheat shipments to Rome. There I was given to understand that the wheat shipments were to be short in tonnage, to double our profit. This had been the custom. Well, finally someone talked; there was a scandal in Rome, and though the senator, who had great influence, began to hand out large bribes to complaining merchants and court officials, he thought it better I should not be questioned in a court. I should vanish until he could safely call me home.

Though only a year had passed since my flight from Jerusalem, I now found myself there again, but this time not as an affluent merchant; I was just a scribe for Pontius Pilate, the Roman governor, a friend of the senator's. I was living in a little stone house high on the hill near the great Roman Antonia fortress. Every day I went to the fortress and worked as a scribe, watching and waiting for the letter from the senator that would call me home. I was avoiding Jews who had been my friends. I stayed with Romans.

When my old friend Ezekiel, the physician, looked me up, I was moved. He told me the priest had taken his wife to Egypt, then he dropped the subject. "Come home with me," he said, and I went. His wife, embracing me, cried, "This is wonderful, Philo. Now Ezekiel can take you to his tailor and have you pick out some decent-looking clothes for him." Pear-shaped Ezekiel always looked sloppy no matter what he wore, but we went to the tailor together. After that day he began to take me to all the houses we used to visit. No one mentioned the priest's wife. It was unnatural, I thought. But I went on living alone in my little stone house, and by the spring-time when the rains came, I was feeling secure.

They say the city lacks water, that stone needs water, but when it keeps raining and rivulets flow down the hills, Jerusalem looks and feels like a big damp tomb. Then, when the rain stops and the dawn comes, the city is radiant in a pure white light. It was on these white mornings that the letters from Rome came every day to the fortress. No letter came for me. I was always there, showing my disappointment.

My friend Marcellus, the captain, who got many let-ters himself, tried gently to rid me of my faith in the senator's promises. Marcellus was a handsome, fastidi-ous soldier with a distinguished air to go with his high forehead and cropped curling hair. He was the bastard son of a member of an old Roman family, and he could talk to me about the poets, preferring Propertius above the others, as I did too, and though he shaved his legs, no soldier dared taunt him. He was too brave, too ruthless a captain. I often rolled the dice with him. He would gamble on anything to see where he stood with the gods.

In his sympathetic woman's tone, he said to me, "I can't understand how it is you don't see that in Rome you would only be an embarrassment to the senator. You're here to stay, my dear Philo, in this land where anything can happen to you. It hurts me to see you so disappointed when I'm the one who gets a letter."

"Yes, I'm disappointed — just for a moment," I replied. "But it's you who are the disappointed man. I feel it in you. What is it, Marcellus?" Laughing, he said cynically, "Of course I'm disappointed. But the whole world runs on disappointment. It shapes all our lives, doesn't it?"

But he had put a doubt in my mind, and I remembered that in the beginning the senator had not wanted his daughter, Livia, to marry me. My father in Crete, convinced that my talents would soon be discovered, had advised me to go to work as the senator's scribe, and I did, and got into his house where I was always near Livia, only sixteen, with long black hair to her shoulders, a golden skin, and wide-set eyes that enchanted me. I used to read her the Greek love poets. My whole life was in that house. It was impossible for me in my menial position to appear in public with her. But when the senator was absent, the house became a rich, opulent world with everything open to us, and at sixteen she was recklessly ardent. She wanted me. We loved. Soon she was pregnant and we both knew the senator would kill me. The nights were heartbreaking. She would beg me to run for my life to Egypt or Crete; I would refuse, insisting that if we had to be separated forever, I preferred it to be by my own death.

When I told the senator she was pregnant by me, his silence frightened me. He was a big, powerful bald-

headed man, and I knew he was ruthless. Suddenly cursing and kicking at me, he ran for his sword. When he
came at me and I did not move, bowing my head, he was
stunned. Drawing back, then sitting down, he stared,
wild-eyed, then rushed out of the room. Next day he
told me I could marry Livia, and he would take me into
one of his great commercial enterprises.

When Livia died in childbirth, he seemed to want to
give all his affection to me because she had loved me. His
respect for me grew with his affection. We trusted each
other. So I didn't thank Marcellus. It seemed to me if I
lost my faith in the senator, I could have no faith in any
of my judgments, and it was my judgment that if I could
keep out of trouble here in Judea I would be back in
Rome by summer's end.

I liked being in the marketplace among the robed
merchants from the desert, the countryside Jews with
small carts pulled by donkeys, merchants from Damascus in bright turbans and colorful robes, and those travellers from Egypt buying for the caravans they would take
to the sea. I liked being among the local Jews who met
there to gossip and argue, as Roman soldiers came buying trinkets at the stalls under the canopies, and rich
Jewish women were carried by on litters. But that day
after the heavy rains a chill had got into my bones; I had
a heavy cold and shouldn't have gone to the marketplace
at all. The sun coming out had shone for an hour, putting strange shimmering shapes and colors on all the
wet stones, but by the time I got there storm clouds
were gathering again on the rim of the hill. As I stood
watching the crowds, a handsome litter carried by four
slave boys circled around me. The woman on the litter
was the rich young widow who had had me trapped with

the young priest's wife, and our eyes met. When she
showed not the slightest sign of recognition, I wondered
uneasily if these people had come to some agreement
about me.

Then I saw Marcellus with three of his Romans at the
corner of a fruit stand, but I was diverted from them by a
loud argument near me. A man in a fine yellow robe
trimmed with blue was being harangued by a tall thin
man with a long narrow face and blazing angry eyes. It
was something to do with religion. The Jews were
always arguing about the correct reading of their religious laws. When the man in the beautiful yellow robe,
retaining his half-amused serenity, turned away, the
thin man, enraged, grabbed at his arm.

"It's blasphemy," he screamed. "You are a blasphemer."
The man in the yellow robe, with an air of patient understanding, answered, "Blasphemy? To ask if God really
needs all this temple blood? Is he really so thirsty for
blood?" and he smiled, and I liked the cut of his beard,
close cropped as it was, coming around his cheek like side-
burns, then meeting his moustache and circling his
mouth and chin.

A little crowd was gathering around the disputants
when an angry female squeal came from the fruit stand
where Marcellus stood with three soldiers. One of them
had put his hand on a girl's bottom and she had whirled
on him, while he tried to look surprised and innocent.
Then the young man with the girl, grabbing a bunch of
grapes from the stand, smashed them in the Roman's
face. A great yell came from the crowd as the Roman
drew his sword. When Marcellus shouted, the soldier
tried to control himself, but he had already jammed the
heel of the sword into the man's face.

His hand on his gushing nose, the young man screamed and screamed. Soon everybody was screaming, and hundreds of Jews came running wildly, and though they could not have seen what had happened, they cursed and spat at the soldiers, who were trying to grab the young man, now screened from them by the angry crowd.

It was raining hard now. Two soldiers were shoved, or thrown or tripped; they fell on their knees in the mud, and people in a chain around the fallen soldiers danced and screamed, their faces full of frenzied ecstasy, their wet beards gleaming as they kicked at their own colored turbans lying in the mud, and at the soldiers.

Then someone cried out, "Listen to me." The young Jew in the yellow robe had jumped up on a fruit stand. In his face and in his voice was such a passion of concern that I was held and moved. "Do not riot," he cried. "Oh, my brothers, you know what a riot means. A Roman slaughter. Remember the Galileans." But someone cried out, "Renegade," and picking up a heavy block of wood from one of the overturned stalls, threw it at him. The block hit him on the head and he lurched and fell off the stand and lay still.

In the strange silence that followed, I could hear the rain falling. The three Roman soldiers joined Marcellus, their swords out. As the rain came down harder the crowd began to disperse, leaving the fallen man alone in a deepening pool. Yet they had all obeyed his warning — so why didn't they help him now? I wondered. Taking the awning from the fruit stand, I made a shelter for him, and drew him under it. Then I sat down beside him and lifted his head to my knee. A great welt was on his forehead. Sitting in the puddle, tapping his cheek gently with the palm of my hand, I tried to revive him, while Marcellus, untroubled by the rain, stood a few feet away, watching us with a sardonic smile. "It's not your business, Philo," he called. "Why can't you leave them alone?" Then he turned and walked away.

The man's eyelids flickered, and in a moment he opened his eyes and looked up at me. Then he touched his head, made a face and sat up slowly. Nothing was said while we sat beside each other in the big pool of water with the rain still drumming on the canvas.

Finally he asked, "Who are you?"

"I'm Philo of Crete."

"A Greek?"

"A Greek. I'm a scribe for Pilate. Who are you?"

"My name is Judas, Judas Iscariot."

"Well, Judas, someone around here doesn't like you. Someone threw that block of wood at you."

"Did you see who?"

"I'm not sure. I think it was the tall thin man who yelled at you...."

"I know him well. See, it's stopped raining," and he stood up carefully. As I did the same, I shivered. I thought Judas could hear my teeth chattering and was ashamed. I wanted to get home. To keep my teeth silent, I tried talking. "He called you a renegade. What did he mean?" "I'll tell you something," he said, and he managed to smile. "It may be hard for a Greek to understand this. The desert is in all Jews. In most of us it remains hidden in some secret place in the heart wherever we go. But that one never left the desert. It's all there in his mind. He'd pull us all back into it if he could." Then he looked at me closely. "Are you all right?" he asked. I told him I had had a bad cold and now in my soaking wet clothes I had caught a chill. I could feel a fever coming on and should get home.

"You helped me," he said gently. "Let me help you."

"How can you help me?"

"My master will help you."

"He's a healer?"

"Yes, a healer."

"No, thank you," I said. "I know about these healers from the hills."

"You make a mistake. But you'll come to see your mistake. It's a power I have," he said, and I didn't laugh, for though he was standing there in his mud-spattered cloak, with a welt on his head, I could believe he was one of those Jews who know they come from another world. But I had started to shiver. "Excuse me," I said, and kept on shivering.

"Come on," he said, taking my arm. "You should be in bed."

At my house, climbing the stairs to my little room with the couch and the desk, nothing was said. Even while he helped me pull off my soaking garments he didn't talk. When I was naked on the couch he threw the covers over me; then, seeing that my teeth still chattered, he tossed every garment hanging on the wall pegs on top of the bed covers. I told him where Ezekiel, my physician, lived. After he had hurried out, I curled up, my eyes closed, and waiting for the first warmth to touch my legs, I lost track of time. When I opened my eyes he was bending over me.

"I talked to your friend, Ezekiel," he said. "He is with a sick woman, but he will come here soon." I felt his hand on my head, cool and comforting, and he seemed to know that I didn't want to talk or open my eyes. So he

talked. He had a good soft voice, soft yet strong, the voice
of a cultivated man. He was born in Cyprus, he said. His
parents wanted him to be a great rabbinical scholar, so
he had studied law and all the great prophetic books, and
being of a philosophical bent, he had read the Greeks and
Romans. But somewhere along the way his mind had
taken another turn. He had become a wanderer, earning
a small living as a tutor, giving help to young scholars in
villages. His disappointed parents cut off the money.

"That's about it," he said, waiting to see if I had fallen
asleep.

"Go on," I mumbled, my head half covered. "Why did
you wander around?"

"I don't know why," he said. "No, I don't. Just that
nothing seemed to be in the right place." He let me wait a
long time, then he said he remembered a day in Jerusalem when he had carried a lamb to the temple for the
sacrificial slaughter and he held the lamb warmly, stroking its head, and wondered idly why God wanted this
poor lamb's throat to be slit so its warm blood would run
on the altar. Then he found himself wondering if there
couldn't be something else that a man could do that
might please God more, and where was God anyway?

Well, his lonely wandering began the day when he
asked where God was. He went to Egypt, he went to
Persia. In Egypt he had loved one woman, and in Persia
there had been a girl he still dreamt of even now. A man
can't control his dreams. And in Damascus he had loved
the young wife of a very rich fat old man who had bought
her from her father. The old man had made her his
prisoner; he was cruel and insanely jealous and she hated
him. "She fled with me from Damascus," he said. They
took ship to an island in the Ionian sea where they were

happy, but there was always a sweet anguish because they knew the happiness couldn't last. On the island was an old Greek scholar who loved Plato, and in the daytime they argued. In the nighttime he had his girl.

But the rich old man, having found out where they were, came in a ship, offering him a large sum of money to leave the girl, and though he could have been rich, he couldn't betray his own heart. In the passing months they fled from one island to another with the old man always finding out where they were, and then one day the old man came with armed men who seized the girl. After beating him, they told him that if ever he came to Damascus he would be killed. He started wandering again, he said, "till one day I was on the road near Bethlehem — "

But then we heard Ezekiel come in. Big sloppy Ezekiel with his soft brown eyes. As I sat up, the fever burning in me may have made everything look misshapen, but Ezekiel had a distant air, as if they had talked, and he, the fashionable physician, had been wounded by Judas's attitude. Or maybe he had found that Judas did not appreciate his very ironic humor.

While I was taking the potion Ezekiel had prepared for me, Judas was saying goodbye. I can't remember what we said. When he had gone I remember Ezekiel asking, "Where did he come from?"

"Where do you come from, Ezekiel?" I mumbled. "Where do you all come from?" I asked with a bright foolish grin, then fell asleep.

For a week I had such a fever I could not tell who came or went, and when the fever broke, I had no desire to get out of bed or to eat. Though I had no fever now, I shivered. Soon I was like a tired old man with no interest in anything going on around me. I think Judas came two or three times to see me, but I had no interest in either Ezekiel or Judas. When I heard them talking, their voices seemed to be far away. But I didn't want to get up.

Late in the afternoon of the sixth day, when Ezekiel was sitting on the bed making witty scandalous remarks about people in high places, trying to get me to laugh with him, Judas came in with a copper-haired girl of eighteen. Paying no attention to Ezekiel, he said, "Philo, this is Mary from Samaria." She came closer, smiling, and as I looked up listlessly at her golden face, she took my hand, then, at a sign from Judas, began to take off her clothes. Outraged at this interference from Judas, my physician strode up and down the room, throwing angry glances at Judas, who paid no attention to him. When the girl was naked she let us all look at her; then she smiled, so sure was she of her body's beauty, and so sure, too, that Judas knew what he was doing. Coming closer to me, she drew back the covers and got into bed with me. As I felt her lips and her tongue on my neck, Ezekiel, muttering to himself, rushed out. A few moments later, Judas, smiling, followed Ezekiel. The girl said nothing. Only when she had curled her warm body around me did she murmur something that told me what I needed. I took her. Then I fell sound asleep.

Later, half awakened by a movement close by, I saw her there in the lamplight, her clothes on now. Bending over, she gently tucked the blankets around me. The lamplight gave her silky skin the sheen of highly burnished copper. Moving delicately she lay down beside me, just to be there, comfortingly near me. When I woke up, I kept my eyes closed. I was marvellously soothed by her nearness. From these harlots a man usually gets only sensual satisfaction, but while she lay on her elbow watching me, thinking she was unobserved, I felt an intimacy I had rarely known with a woman.

In the morning when I woke up, I watched her preparing a big bowl of soup. She had brought some fruit and wine and cheese. I got up and ate with her. Her ease with me was astonishing. She couldn't have known much about me, but whatever it was, she knew it with a smiling certainty.

"Where is your friend Judas?" I asked.

"I don't know."

"Does he have you sleep with him? How well do you know him?"

"Last year he came to my village to instruct my young brother. My mother liked him. He's not like those farmers. He's very patrician, isn't he? He knew I was here in Jerusalem." I was so busy marvelling at the satisfaction she took in her own beauty I didn't notice that she hadn't told me whether Judas used her himself. It was as if her beauty was such a bottomless purse that she could afford to be generous and share it with others.

When I was about to pay her from the stock of silver I kept hidden in my room, she told me she planned to stay for some months in Jerusalem and make some money. Looking at her, I didn't know how to explain the pang I felt, so I fumbled around, asking her to tell me about her family. She had a mother and two little sisters, she said, whom she tried to keep in comfort. A young merchant had assured her she would grow rich in Jerusalem, she said, and I was upset again, knowing that when a whore has no place of her own, and no independence, she goes downhill fast and becomes pitiful.

Then I couldn't bear to think of this girl losing the

spirit that so renewed me. I couldn't let her leave me. I kept her all day, waiting, expecting Judas to come so I could talk to him about her. When he didn't come I kept asking myself how he could be so certain I would want to keep her. Nor could Mary tell me where I could find him. By this time, she said, he might be off somewhere in the countryside with his healer, who now seemed to take up his whole life. I asked her to stay the night. We negotiated. She stayed.

Next day at noontime, just when she was going out to shop for food, Ezekiel, who was coming in, bumped into her at the door. Hearing me laugh, he was taken aback. Or maybe Mary's manner, lighthearted, casual, and neighborly, annoyed him. He was an established physician and she was just a whore. Now that the rain had ended, wasn't the sunlight wonderful? she said, then she was gone, and Ezekiel, flopping heavily on a little chair, tried taking a mocking tone. "I can see why I was dismissed as your physician," he said. And then, shrugging, "I was, you know. That man Judas what's-his-name took charge," and though he smiled, there was an edge on his voice. "Who does he think he is?"

"Oh, come on, Ezekiel," I laughed. "Of course he should have consulted you. But he was carried away."

"No, he wasn't. He doesn't care what I think."

"Were you really so annoyed, Ezekiel?"

"Of course I was annoyed. I'm your physician. Who is he, anyway?"

I told how I had met Judas and how he had stood atop the fruit stand, crying out to the angry crowd, and how I had been struck by his bearing and the light in his face — as if there was a fire in his head, and how he had moved me, and yet one man had called out "renegade."

"Renegade. Oh, I see," he said with satisfaction.

"I have a feeling about that man, Ezekiel."

"So have I, Philo. I talked to him. Yes, indeed, we talked a lot."

"Where was this?"

"Right here in this room while you were dozing," he said, and as he fell silent, remembering, his whole expression changed. "Look, Philo," he said, "it's enough for me that I'm a Jew."

"And it's not enough for him?"

"No."

"Is it supposed to be enough for me that I'm a Greek?"

"It's quite a different thing," he said. "You wouldn't understand."

And then with an impatient gesture, changing the subject, he asked if the girl had moved in with me. I said she hadn't, but I knew I needed her; her freshness quickened me, and I couldn't bear to think of her practicing her trade here in the city at the beck and call of brutish men, and I wondered if I could set her up in some little place of her own. At first Ezekiel laughed at me, then he grew interested. "Well, it might keep you away from the wives of those priests," he said, startling me. It was the first time he had mentioned the priest's wife.

But wouldn't my friend Judas have something to say? he asked, since he had the girl in hand. I insisted Judas was just her good friend, a family friend. He grinned at this. Then we tried to think of a suitable place near by. Finally he asked me if I had noticed a little stone house outside the west wall and near the inn, a little place that had been vacant for some time. In the end we went to see it.

II

I furnished this place with carpets, silks, and pottery and a lovely couch in the smaller room. It was not cheap, and I asked myself why the senator was not sending money since he should have been looking after me, but then, a connection might have been discovered. Anyway, I provided Mary with a little maid, and whenever I got away from the officials at the Antonia I would ride out to the little house near the inn.

Her affection was growing. She would ask me to stay overnight and came close to tears when I couldn't. I knew she had all the tricks of the bed, but I believed I had touched some natural warmth that surged up and left her exhausted, curled beside me like a very young girl. Yet I suspected she had other clients, and once I tried to find out, casually, taking a light tone, but she clawed at me and I was so confused I slapped her face. Stunned, she stared at me. "You slapped me," she whispered.

At one moment she might be off by herself in a long, contented silence, and a few minutes later, if there was a little quarrel, she would burst into angry tears, her eyes clouded with murderous rage. I wanted to give her presents but I couldn't afford them. I was ashamed. I told her about the senator, how I was still in his service and would soon be asked to return to Rome, where I would have a rich, expensive life. I told her I couldn't bear to see myself back in Rome without her. She would be with me in Rome. I don't think she believed me.

I liked walking with her into the village to get food. I liked the arrogant security she found in her own beauty. One day there was a sudden sun shower, the sun shining through light rain on her head and face, and I knew I had never been happier. Something in her, secret and hidden, kept pulling me to her, but I was needed in Caesarea.

In Caesarea, I wrote letters for Pilate to officers at the Antonia, to the high priest and certain elders of the Sanhedrin, who collaborated with us. I was to carry these back to Jerusalem.

It was a spring morning. Marcellus, on patrol with his small troop of twelve men, asked me to ride beside him. My horse, a mare, was snorting and circling, her tail high in the early sunlit spring air, as if she were in season. The troop moved out and I, mounting last in the sour reek of manure in the stable, saw a stocky red-haired man alone at the entrance to the yard, staring at me. The strong sunlight fell on his face and I saw that he had only one ear.

My horse walked so close this fellow had to step aside, and yet he never took his eyes off me. I turned, a tightening around my heart, and in my mind I saw his ear on the ground and me kneeling in the moonlight looking down at it. Yet this man didn't even blink. Nothing was said.

Riding up to Marcellus, I wondered if the man was keeping track of me for the priest in Egypt. Then, maybe
because the morning air was so bright, I decided I'd seen
a good omen. Even if he was the one who had tried to kill
me, he showed no recognition, as if it were agreed that
nothing was to be said about me and the priest's wife.
But how could it have been arranged?

As our troop rode along I kept wondering why Marcellus looked younger. He usually indulged himself in
Caesarea, where every pleasure, every dissipation, was
available to the Romans. Yet, he had happily held himself
in check. "You look well, Marcellus," I said. Coming
closer, so close I could have touched him, he gave a happy
laugh without the sound of the laugh and said, "Do you
know something, Philo? For the first time in two years
I'm in love." Marcellus was a handsome man. The frank-
ness in his eyes, the open pleasure in his face, made me
feel good in his company on that dusty road. I did not ask
him if he loved a boy or a girl. I tried to understand such
new sweet untroubled happiness because Marcellus had
had a terrible life, his wife committing suicide when he
turned away from her and brought boys to the house.
His family had paid him to stay far away, and though he
masked his bitterness with a strange mixture of tough-
ness and charm, he could be cruel. And yet there he was
with that happy, soundless laugh and the sun on his
forehead, riding in the Judean hills, almost beautiful in
the radiance of his contentment.

At high noon, resting by a well in the shade of olive
trees, we ate, and fed and watered the horses. The sun,
as always, was brutally direct, and for hours a dust-laden
wind from the desert cut my face. The horses needed

rest and lots of water. Marcellus asked how I had liked working for Pilate in Caesarea. I said I'd be glad to be back in Jerusalem.

Then, moving on, we heard screams up ahead and rounded a bend to see a caravan being attacked by robbers; in those days the hills were full of patriotic thieves. Three of the caravan's guards lay dead, and a merchant staggered around in a circle clutching at his side. Four other merchants were backing away from the loaded wagons. As Marcellus and his troops charged down the road, one of the bandits shouted and they all ran to their horses, which were untethered just off the road. But one horse, excited by the shouts, broke away and galloped for the hills, leaving one bandit circling around horseless until he swung up behind another rider. And then, with an exultant wave they rode across the wide field by an olive grove, with our troop in pursuit.

They kept to a narrow trail, avoiding the wooded hills. The trees thinned out and the landscape changed, and soon there was only scrub and jutting barren crags, low cliffs, great rocks, dead things, and fleeing horsemen on the edge of the desert. I was appalled by the lonely glare of desolation, but Marcellus cried out, "They don't think we dare follow them. This wilderness is their sanctuary."

Our horses were freshly watered and one of theirs was burdened by two men. I was sure we'd catch them, but a wind came up, low dark clouds hid the sun, and then the rising sand began to swirl around us, blowing fiercely, trying to drive us back. It blew harder, but we kept going, coming up over a high ridge where we saw a figure on foot, beside a writhing horse. Lurching down the slope of stone rubble he looked like the loneliest man on earth. Marcellus merely pointed. Two soldiers rode at the lone staggering Jew. He drew his sword and as he waited in his terrible isolation I cried to Marcellus, "He's your prisoner."

"Bandits are not prisoners."

The soldiers slashed at the man's neck. He fell. There was a pool of blood on the sand. I don't know why I dismounted but as I went closer, Marcellus shielded his face with his cloak and watched me. The Jew was young, and as he lay with his cheek softly cradled on the sand, I heard him sigh, and then he dug his fingers deep into the grit as if trying to draw the desert into him in a last desperate embrace. And I thought of Judas saying, "The desert is in all of us, hidden somewhere in the heart." Shaken, I watched the sand cake in his gaping mouth.

"Philo," Marcellus said. "I think you spend too much time with Jews."

"It's a Jewish place, Marcellus."

Leaning forward in the saddle to look down on the dead man, he said, "In Rome, there was always a Jew, attractive, a pet, an exotic, a charmer. But I never got involved, deeply involved, with a Jew without in the end knowing that something had been lost."

The soldiers dismounted, led their horses towards us, and as the wind howled, all light fading in the sandstorm, we lay down close together, shielding our faces with our cloaks. I could feel the covering sand, warm like a light blanket and keeping out the sudden awful cold, and then the blanket became so heavy I thought I would be smothered. My sense of isolation from the world was so bewildering I felt a terrible need to touch someone else, bring someone close to me, and when I reached out, a hand touched my own arm, as if we knew we could only survive holding on to each other, keeping everything else out. I closed my eyes to the terror in this land of sharp sunlight, the wind, and the hidden dark desert. It struck me that perhaps the senator wanted me back in Judea where anything could happen, where the land would rid him of me, but I couldn't believe my father-in-law wanted to get rid of me.

Suddenly the moan in the wind died away into silence, and when this stillness remained unbroken, we clawed out of the sand, coughing, shaking our cloaks, to find a new strange light in the air. I couldn't see any sign of the dead bandit in the level sand, and the sun came filtering through the dusty air, and then, almost too abruptly, there were streaks of brilliant sunlight, and just over-head a huge hanging pink flower of light, its beauty bewildering.

By the time we had made out way back to the high-way, stars were out. Marcellus decided to camp in a farmer's field. We built a fire, and got food from the farmer, paying him well. And in the morning we moved on toward the city. The road was one of the ten great highways leading to the walls, crowded with farmers in carts, and goat-herders and hundreds of children scram-bling on the bald stone hills like flies, the flies that were always on their own olive faces; tens of thousands had been on this road, and they brought with them a huge cloud of dust and a rotten stench that still hung over the city and the great rebuilt city walls.

My mind was full of the desert, and I felt I had never seen this city so clearly as a place whose people had their hearts and minds first shaped by that wilderness. There it was, crusted on the two great hills, small stone houses twisted tier after tier on the slopes, a city all of stone, splintered rock scalded and gleaming in the sunlight, taking on a metallic glitter, yellow, ivory, and saffron. Suddenly startled, I halted and stared; the city was a great yellow flower, a beautiful picture, a picture in stone.

Yet, no living things were represented in stone in this city. Even their desert god had no human face, and I let Marcellus get ahead, remembering something my father had told me, mounted on his own horse. "Yes, in the desert there's a facelessness, Philo, and it should be utterly alien to your nature." A physician in Crete, he had tutored me himself, and even trained me to use the short sword. I could see him one day sitting by a stream, telling me to watch water flowing over the pebbles, telling me that even the most abstract thoughts must be concrete, and that life as a river was only one view; and then, after a long reflective silence, he said, smiling to himself, "Yes, golden Cynthia in Tibur's ground."

He got up, and we walked more than a mile to some ruins, many of them just great stone slabs, and he told me that these slabs had been thrown up by the sea, that long ago there had been an island off the coast of Crete and now there were legends about the people of Thera and about these slabs, cleaned and restored so we could see their paintings. And the happiness, the satisfaction, in my father's face made me want to see what he saw. I looked hard at the paintings and in a little while, lifted out of myself, I shared my father's wonder. "There's something Egyptian there, yes," he said, "but they're quite different, the musical rhythms in a gaiety of flowers, a sweet harmony of life. You must learn about Aristotle, yes, but look at these paintings, there it all is, Philo. Remember it."

There, outside Jerusalem, Marcellus kept turning,

wondering what was keeping me, and suddenly he slapped his horse and galloped off. I had been deliberately holding back because on this side of the Gihan wall there was Mary's little house, up the road, and approaching the house I felt a sudden sensual arousal and also the old fear, a deep foreboding that I would see a man coming out of the house. And somehow I imagined my own fury, as if it could be a cleansing, if a man actually was there. But she was alone, alone at the door and full of surprise and beautiful in her yellow robe. She prepared a bath, and when I was in the water she said, "Judas was here looking for you."

"Then it's known you're here."

"He stayed around for a while."

"A little while?"

"He had friends waiting for him."

"Good friends don't mind waiting," I said.

"They didn't look like him, or the kind of friends he'd have. They looked like farmers or fishermen."

"What did he say about me?"

"He said he liked you."

"That's all?"

"He said something about you being open — or having an open mind — I think that was it."

She was bathing me, the touch so soothing and delightful I forgot about the sandstorm and the wild desert storm-flower.

III

The way that young Jew had died in the desert must have remained in the back of my mind, for now I began to notice little things in Jerusalem I hadn't noticed before. Walking in the streets with Roman friends and passing groups of Jews, old or young, I saw things in their faces, things that had to be caught in a first quick glance before they vanished quickly in amiable friendly greetings — dreams of suddenly rising and massacring the Romans. Underneath the good will they remained hard, ruthless, warlike, and full of wounded pride. I had always liked Jerusalem, but never felt any sense of real tranquillity there. The collaboration between the Romans and the Sanhedrin, backed as it was by the rich merchants, who did great business even in the worst of times, was despised by many factions. No matter how happy the collaboration appeared to be, I felt they were always waiting, even the very old, just remembering and waiting.

At this time I was busy preparing reports from officials, getting them ready for Pilate and the troops who would be in Jerusalem at the time of the great Passover festival, when a hundred thousand, coming in from the countryside, would be full of national fervor. I was working hard, but in the late afternoons, when my work was finished, I would ride out to see Mary, who sometimes asked me to stay overnight. I was happy then, for surely by this time I could tell when a woman really wanted a man near her and when a kind of fulfillment and peace comes into her body. My happiness was all mixed up with wonder that she now could be satisfied with me alone. Is it possible, just possible, for a woman to forget she is a whore? Mary was young enough to forget, young enough to be unaware she was changing, always becoming something else. She kept coaxing me to go with her to Samaria and meet her mother and tell her about the life we planned in Rome.

But instead of going to Samaria I was ordered to go to Jericho to take depositions from merchants who had charged the local tax collector with bribery and corruption. I was to leave with a caravan that was taking the Jericho road. The night before leaving, I was at Ezekiel's house, a fine stone house with a lovely garden in the upper city, for dinner and conversation. Some wives were there, and Ezekiel had told me to make myself agreeable to the big fat wheezing merchant Joab, who had a golden touch, and who could easily put me in the way of making some money in Damascus, where he had large holdings. I talked to him as a man who had been a great merchant. I hinted that I would like to see him in his own house. But I knew that no foreign merchant — Roman, Greek, or Egyptian — ever got into his home.

Yet, he did great business with them. How he got away with it fascinated me. But the others, the three young priests, the four merchants and their pretty wives, loved all the Greek things, and we could have had an Athenian evening, but as soon as I had eaten I felt exhausted. My head began to swim and I said I needed a little air and would step into the garden.

A cool little breeze in the garden rustled the palm leaves, and brought a faint stench from the temple neighborhood. I could never get used to that smell of blood. As I stood looking down over the tiered city, all in moonlight now, the things of the desert must have been still with me, or maybe my head was still swimming, but looking down into the valley, I wondered if the desert demons had come here too and made the valley their home and at this hour were gathering and waiting for the real midnight dark to come and free them so they could roam around the city, stealing into houses and bedrooms, seeking the ruin of unwary men and women who had forgotten to wear the little silver bells that ward off demons. I had been told I should be wearing these barbarous bells myself. Barbarous? Love's silver bells! Are they ever barbarous? Anyway, I couldn't believe a demon was always at my elbow waiting for me to make one wrong turn. And Judas, the one who talked to me about the desert being always there in a secret place in the Jewish heart — what would he say about demons and the bells, if I called them love's silver bells?

"Philo, are you there?" asked a young woman's voice. "Do you feel better, Philo? I can't see you."

"I'm over here," I called, but couldn't take my eyes off the valley below, for I had just remembered that the city gates were locked at night. No matter how desperate my need, now no one from outside could get in to see me. I felt utterly confined and alone.

A man laughed, a loud happy laugh, in the house.

And why think of Judas? I wondered. What did I know of the man? Just a general impression. A superior man. A few things said that excited my imagination. A sense that so much more would soon be said. Then again that woman's voice, the soft eyes in that voice, "Philo?" Why did only women call me? And I still didn't take my eyes from the valley, and when I heard another laugh in the house, a young man's laugh, I thought of that young Jew dying in the desert. I heard again the lonely shriek as he fell, utterly alone, the sand caressing his cheek as he caressed the sand. Only now the wail seemed to come from the valley below, and I felt a power coming not from the house alone, but from all around me in the moonlit city, a power pushing at me, pushing me away, a desert power pushing, telling me everything I wanted was outside the walls, and to get out and leave them as they wanted to be — walled in. I've had too much wine, I thought, and I went in. I told them I had to go home and get some rest. In the morning I was journeying to Jericho.

I travelled with four merchants, four armed guards, and a rich baggage wagon, travelling slowly and with some delays. Just before midnight we stopped for some rest in a clearing back from the highway cutting through the deep valley. Our four guards, tough experienced Jewish mercenaries, built a fire and sat around while the four merchants and I slept. A terrible clattering, clanging, and banging woke me. Scared out of my wits by wild shrieks coming out of the hills I jumped up, then crouched by the wagon wheel while the guards ran around the wagon, sometimes darting into the shadows, only to return.

Like the rest of us they were stunned by the sudden utter silence. Then from high on the hill came one awful lonely wail. Then the silence again. Shivering, I stared at the moon. Even the guards were moonstruck. Suddenly there was a great shrieking — it was all around us. Men came leaping out of the shadows — dozens of them, I thought. Our guards, standing together near the fire, knocked two of them down. One of the merchants, drawing his sword, slashed at a bandit running around the wagon, and another bandit, coming up behind the merchant, killed him with one blow. Motionless, close to the wheel, I was half hidden and that gave me time to draw my short sword — I had no fear of any one of them if I could get him alone.

But then I saw a big man come leaping out of the shadows into the firelight where the guards were driving back six men, and with his long curved sword he took on the four guards by himself. One of the guards shrieked and fell. The other three fled into the trees, and I saw there weren't more than ten bandits. This powerful one, their leader, was there in the firelight. The light flickered on his battered old Roman helmet, and he wore pants with thongs around the legs like a Gaul. Putting up my sword, I stepped away from the wagon into the firelight, and with a shrug held up my arms. The three merchants joined me.

Even in the moonlight it was plain this broad-shouldered, big-muscled man with the great black beard and the fierce eyes enjoyed his work. He was laughing. This rattled the merchants. But I took on a calm and dignified air when he began to question us. I was not a merchant, I said. I often translated for Pilate himself; I would be missed. I tried to be quiet and distant, hoping to put fear of Roman vengeance in him, but when I had finished, he said something like, "Well, well, well," his hands on his hips, grinning, and passed on to the others. Finally he released the terrified merchants. He had them stripped of everything, even their coats. "Take them away," he said, and took me back to his camp. What happened to the merchants, I don't know. I suppose they were killed.

"You come with me," he said and took me deeper in the hills and let me sit by the fire and warm myself. It gets cold in those hills. It was plain he was no thug but a man of some education who was very much at ease with himself. He took off the helmet, revealing a dome-like forehead. He wanted to know about Roman troop movements. He asked me to name friends I had in high places. I threw out important names, many names, and kept on till I saw my pretensions were amusing him. His ease as he studied me coldly, and the power I felt in him, began to frighten me. He was now sitting cross-legged by the fire, his head back, and he hardly turned when we heard a scream. I turned, waiting. I was sure one of the merchants was dying.

I got nervous. I felt that if I could make myself seem important I would be kept alive, so I started talking about my close friendship with Pilate. While I talked like this I really felt important, far too important to die in these hills. "So you might be good for a ransom," he said, brightening. Thinking of course of the senator, I went to mention him. Then with a chilling sense of uncertainty I checked myself.

I could see the senator at home, a ransom letter in his

hand, his big handsome face troubled as he pondered, then, standing up, began to pace up and down in his bare feet. He never wore sandals in the house. I used to keep my eyes on his bare feet whenever he was troubled. Each of the big, blunt-toed heavy feet seemed to say he would have his own way. Now as he paced up and down I could see regret in his face. He was really fond of me, he really would like to have had me back with him if the coast were clear — especially since I had taken the blame and agreed to vanish. He was corrupt, but no more corrupt than his colleagues, and among corrupt men who know each other there is great loyalty. My death at the hand of bandits would not be of his doing, nor would it be something he wanted. Not asked for! Just given, and he would be free of me, and he would not feel he was betraying me. A sense of betrayal would depend on the depth of his affection for me. If there was no real love, he could never feel he had betrayed himself. This, then, was a business matter. Money for a vanished witness who was still evidently an embarrassment to him....

And all my faith in him faltered, and as another screech came from the bushes, I felt utterly alone, in my chest suddenly a terrible tightness, and I said desperately, "Wait a minute," holding him while my wits worked to save my life. I told him I might be worth far more to him in Jerusalem than any ransom he could get for me. I was no Roman. I was a Greek. And if he could be told the time of the departure of rich caravans and the routes to be taken . . . I talked on till I realized he was no longer listening. His head back, he was watching the night sky, watching with such patient intensity I felt a little chill on my neck, realizing he wasn't stargazing and lost in meditation about me; he was reading the stars and the reading might take a long time, and my fate was in the reading.

For me the starlit sky is a beautiful tapestry wrapped around the earth. There is order and harmony in the heavens, and even the constellations show the gods taking the forms of bears, or lions or other things here on earth, and everything is in a harmony of place. But this man was not of my world, nor were his stars. Never shifting his body, staring intently and patiently, he read the heavens with that star wisdom of this land whose people had great lore in these matters thousands of years before the Jews came out of the desert. While he watched and read, he became like a native of this old star-haunted land. By this time his own father might have forgotten the intricate methods of the science of the ancient master astronomers who had their under-standing of the relationship of the heavenly bodies to us, and he wouldn't be able to explain it either, but this method was in the blood. This one could read — without knowing how he read — each flicker of light from a fixed or moving star. Each star told him something about his destiny, and maybe something new about me, while I waited in the dreadful silence of these lonely hills. I had never felt so far from home or so much at the mercy of a wisdom I did not understand.

Suddenly he said, "I believe you. Let's talk." Leaving the fire, he got two leather wine bags from his tent. But even while we drank, he said little. We still required more silence in the dark to find some peculiar recognition of each other. Finally he began to talk. He told me he was Simon, the Idumaean, and only half Jewish, like the great Herod. In his Idumaea to the south, his family, once rich and important, had been dispossessed in the wars. When he stirred up the embers of the fire, and the flames shot up, flickering on his great bearded head, so that his face seemed to come flashing at me out of the darkness, I marvelled at my sudden confidence in him. And though his men slept in their blankets near by, we could have been alone in the Judean hills.

He asked me to tell him more about my life in Rome; some day he wanted to go there himself. Moreover, he had a question about Roman women. The fire had burned so low I could hardly see him, just hear the voice in the darkness asking if Roman women were all short-legged; he had got this impression looking at so many of those clay figurines — little pottery portraits so common in Rome and left everywhere the Romans went, many of them in full figure. All the women short-legged, he said. He liked a woman to have slim long legs like his own wife. I finally had to agree he had made an interesting point well worth looking into. It was perhaps a matter of the waist. High-waisted girls. Low-waisted girls. He was lucky the gods had looked after him and given him a high-waisted girl.

But he didn't count on the gods looking after him, he said. He had learned to count only on himself, which was very satisfactory; in the long run a man had only his own self-respect to fall back on, and since he understood this, he was free from the Jewish law which put a grip on a man even in his dreams, and free, too, from any allegiance to Roman law, and as he went on I became intoxicated by the sense of freedom I felt in him — so rare in Judea. Impulsively I put out my hand. We made a bargain. Then he took me to his tent, telling me his young wife travelled with him and shared his lot, and he woke her. In the dark I could see the whites of her eyes, the eyes never leaving me as he told her I would be his friend, and she said not a word.

Returning to the fire, we talked about the situation in Judea. Other bandits in the countryside offered themselves as messiah patriots, bent on delivering Jerusalem, and since they robbed in the name of the god of Israel, they were often heroes in Jerusalem, where they could count on support from many lower priests. But not him, not Simon, the Idumaean. The others were thieves, just as he was. They looted and robbed just to fill their own purses or to become powerful, hoping some day to make themselves kings. Not him. He was an outlaw. In such a land at such a turbulent time when it was fashionable to talk about the approaching end of the world, a man owed it to his own self-respect to be an outlaw, didn't I agree? And I did! The man was fascinating me, but I knew it. And the fact was, I was still alive, and had made him treat me with respect. But I wondered how much longer I could get away with it, and what would happen when the fire went out, and the talk ran out, and it was daylight.

He didn't wait. He woke two of his men, two muscular, middle-aged hard-faced men, the one with the great scar on his cheek called Isaiah, son of James, and the other, a squat powerful man with enormous shoulders, John of Jericho. "Remember this man," he said to them. "Be loyal to him, when you meet him in Jerusalem." While they eyed me, both of them grim and suspicious, I told them they could meet me in the marketplace, or in the outer court of the temple, or Simon himself might come to that inn on the high road just beyond the West Gate near the first olive grove. I told them I could meet them tomorrow in the marketplace, late in the afternoon.

They kept on eyeing me silently, letting Simon wait. Finally, they took him aside and began to argue with him. It was an angry argument; I gathered they were refusing to meet me in Jerusalem and let themselves be captured and killed. In the end Simon silenced them. Soon they were standing quietly behind him.

"They don't think I understand you. Well, I know I do," he said.

"I'm sure you do," I said.

"And I know I'm right about you."

"You know and I know," I said.

"If I'm wrong, Philo, I'll have your throat cut," and he smiled. "It'll be easy. You are not a Roman soldier, you know. You walk alone in the streets. We have friends there, and some night . . . but it won't happen, will it?" and he put out his hand. "Tomorrow — a nice fat caravan," he said. "Now take a horse," and I did.

As the horse picked its way carefully down the hill in the dark I listened nervously for following footsteps and thought of Simon saying, "I know I'm right about you," and couldn't believe I had talked my way out. It didn't occur to me at this time that he could have meant that he recognized how corrupt a man I was.

When the horse reached the road I let out an exultant yell and gave him a slap and rode at a wild gallop, all by myself in the dawn light. And I couldn't stop wondering how so wise and shrewd a man as this Simon could be so foolish as to believe what I said, or what any man will say with a knife at his throat. And soon I could see the great West Gate shining in the first sunlight which was yellowing the stone houses atop the hills.

At the gate I told the officer about the raid on the caravan and about my escape. The officer cursed Simon.

For weeks, he said, they had been trying to trap him in those hills. After resting the horse I rode slowly through the deserted streets and up the hill to the stables. There I also told a stablehand about the raid. I couldn't tell him I had been given the horse; the telling would be too complicated, so I said I had stolen the horse and escaped. Then, crossing the courtyard and entering the fortress, I asked the first young officer I met if Lepidus, the garrison commander, was awake, and if he could also bring Marcellus to the commander; it was necessary that I see them. After a long wait I was taken to the quarters of Lepidus, who was eating. Sitting with him, picking at some grapes in a table bowl, was Marcellus; his hand going out to the grapes was not like a soldier's hand.

For months this Lepidus with a big square face and brown blotches on the forehead and a pompous manner had been irritating me profoundly. The Lepidus Commentaries — that's what they would be called by posterity, he was sure — were dull and graceless as he wrote them, but he still had me working on them, rewriting them. "You have the touch, Philo," he would whisper. "Give them your own style, your polish, and some wit," and I think I hated him for making me do it.

As soon as I sat down with Lepidus and Marcellus I was touched by a strange secret excitement. Even though I was exhausted I felt it. I told them the truth. I told them how I had sat talking to Simon and, somehow gaining his confidence, had persuaded him I could serve him here in Jerusalem with information about the routes of the caravans. I told them two of his thugs would be meeting me tomorrow afternoon in the marketplace. When I had finished, Marcellus looked at Lepidus, who stared at me, then they stared at each other, and then as

they turned to me again their faces were full of astonished admiration. "Philo, you have the golden tongue,
the gift of words," Lepidus said. "But come on, Philo,
admit you stole the horse," put in Marcellus.

"No, he gave me the horse, Marcellus."

"Oh, come on, Philo."

"The horse is there in the stable," I insisted.

"I, too, think you stole the horse," Lepidus said, laughing. "You don't mean to say you believe they'll meet you
here tomorrow?"

"I do," I said.

"Would they be such fools?" Lepidus asked.

"Yes, why should they be such fools?" Marcellus
asked. "They know they'd be seized."

"Of course," Lepidus said, and then, still smiling, he
turned to Marcellus. "Philo is a persuasive man. He has
the golden tongue, and though I can't believe this will
happen, there's just a chance..." And then, though they
couldn't believe Isaiah and John would come into Jerusalem, to be on the safe side they made a plan. Some soldiers could be moving around the marketplace. I would
be given a whistle; if the two bandits approached me, or
if I saw them, I would give a signal. Though they con-
gratulated me on my resourcefulness, Marcellus even
embracing me, I knew they thought I was naïve and gull-
ible about my own powers of persuasion, and I resented
it. I left them to get some sleep.

Late in the afternoon next day, after talking to Marcellus, I was in the marketplace, moving among the stalls
and chatting with merchants, some of them with great
wagons of their own laden with goods. I saw Marcellus
only once, standing with another Roman near a stall
dealing in fine leather work. And I saw him toss a coin

into the pouch of a half-blind old beggar, a patch over one eye, and with a wooden stump for a leg, squatting on the ground at one end of the stall. At the other end was another beggar, whose hands had been chopped off. A dog was asleep at his feet. It was like any other sunny day in the marketplace, and I couldn't be sure any Romans were watching.

Then shadows began to lengthen. People were leaving for their homes. Even the half-blind beggar had got up, picking up his crutch, hobbling around, getting his bearings. The other beggar hadn't moved, though the dog was now licking his face. Then Marcellus, coming from nowhere, said smiling, "Well, they're not the fools you think they are, Philo," and he patted me on the back. "See you tonight, Philo." I was left there, unwatched, I was sure. The merchants were closing up their stalls and the wagons were leaving. Then the beggar, the one without hands, was getting to his feet, the dog pulling on the thong that tied him to a handless arm. I felt foolish and humiliated as I began to leave myself.

Then I heard a clump, clump, clump, a regular hurried pounding on the cobblestones behind me. The hammering worried me. As I turned uneasily, I saw the half-blind old beggar with the crutch and the wooden stump lurch off balance and slide to the ground, and I heard him call out to me. Anyone watching could have seen that with his outstretched hand he was pleading for me to help him to his feet. Bending over him, I was repelled by his smelly rags and his matted hair. Then he brushed back the hair from his face and grinned. His one uncovered eye was bright with amusement. I whispered, "Simon. You here . . . you yourself?"

"Why not?" he said, still grinning, now on his haunches.

"You're crazy," I said, trying not to look around.

"I can't get used to this stump," he said. I knew he must have had the leg hooked back at the knee under the robe. "Here, help me up," and as I got him to his feet and we looked at each other, our eyes meeting, there was a strange silent moment of recognition that filled me with wonder. At that moment I was as sure of him as he was of me, and with his eye and smile he seemed to be offering me again that sense of freedom — a freedom only the artist knows — that he had offered me two nights ago in the hills, only much more compelling now.

"What news did you pick up, Philo?" he asked, shifting around, still giving the appearance of a crippled man trying to get his bearings. My heart was beating heavily, I was so excited. I whispered to him about a caravan leaving for Damascus tomorrow, information I had picked up from a merchant on one of the wagons.

Simon said, "At the week's end in the afternoon be at the inn up the road from the gate, if you can. You'll get your share. We can talk, a good talk — oh, I do love talking to you, Philo. Better get going now, eh?" and even as I left, still tingling with excitement, and hurrying, I wondered why he seemed like my own kin, and what it was in me that made me feel this way. Baffled, yet charmed, I wondered if I felt this way because I was a Greek. Had I long felt secretly that I was a Roman captive? I wondered. And as my thoughts whirled around, I wondered too, if this was why the Jews, another captive people, fascinated me. Those hook-nosed, unattractive-looking people, Marcellus called them. I didn't know.

But I did know this; I now was a criminal, and knowing it only excited me.

IV

Sometimes he came disguised as a travelling merchant, sometimes as a wandering beggar with a tall hooked staff, but often he met me at the inn. Even if a Jew had recognized Simon, he would not have betrayed him; I never found out whether the inn-keeper himself knew who Simon was. The more I learned about Simon the more I liked him and the more often I wanted to be with him, not just because he scrupulously gave me my share of the coin he got from disposing of the loot in distant towns, but because I had come to enjoy his company.

I ate with him at the inn, and eating, I suffered. The man ate like a pig, with never a word while he gobbled his food, smacking his lips, chewing and chomping and belching and really wounding me because I couldn't understand how a man with his natural intelligence, his natural wisdom and grace of perception, could be so indifferent to my sensibilities. I knew I was really his man, his prisoner, and couldn't leave him. But I had utterly unreal conversations with him about soon being back in Rome at a word from the senator, and Simon went along with me. Talk to me, talk to me, Simon, I pleaded with my eyes, for when he was eating I couldn't see him in my Roman dream. I had to pray that he would finish gulping down his food so I could feel my thoughts soaring again as he asked all the right questions about a man's life, questions Pilate himself might have asked, these questions coming out of his own life, which was always so close to death. He must have had a noble family training in Idumaea, so perhaps his eating habits were a revolt against the ritual eating formalities of the Jews.

"You risk death here, Simon," I said to him one day. "Aren't you afraid of death?"

I remember his look of astonishment. "How can you ask this, my friend?" he said. "Death is no stranger to me. Death is a part of me. It can't come at me. I keep death in me half asleep in its secret place where it has been from the time of my birth. I'm death's territory. Death, a little garrison in the territory. Sooner or later it wakes and takes over all its territory. But it's my own garrison, it's my own death," and he laughed.

I had rarely heard a Jew talk about death and what it was. They just died and were buried, although I know that some of them, the Pharisees, for instance, believe in a hereafter. Or so they say. But I have heard that in most ancient times none of them believed in a life beyond the grave. A man died into the tribe. The tribe alone survived, which was why it was sacred. But like all men I wonder if I will ever see my father again. I know that when I die I'll be taken by Hermes into a cloud, all mist and water, and wafted over the great sea toward the river I must cross. Since the clouds are always above and near us, and men and women die every minute of the day, the journeying dead must be all around us.

Yet I wonder sometimes if part of the great sensual sea isn't hidden deep within me, back of my own mind, as the fierce desert always is in the Jews, and in this sea within me are all the sea monsters and great half-hidden rocks, and all the lovely sea sirens luring me on to the end with the taste of ecstasy in the little deaths. But when the sea is crossed, and I come to the river, will I find no one there I love, and will I find that as soon as I am on the river what is really me is lost forever? Then I tell myself that the sea needs the river as the river needs the sea. The river flows back to the sea, and what is still on the river must come back too. I would have told this to Simon, but knew he would shrug and say I was a Greek. I was so carried away by this unreality in my relationship with him that I seemed to forget he had a rope around my neck, and I could raise my glass to him and say, "May the time soon come when I return to Rome and you are rich enough to bring your wife with you. You'll be right at home, for Rome is full of great thieves." While we talked travellers came into the inn, travellers covered with heavy dust from the highway, each one with a parched look from the cruel sun and that harsh desert dust, making me remember the splashing water in the Roman fountains.

One day, leaving the inn to join Isaiah and John, who waited as always with the horses, Simon asked what I knew about a Galilean named Jesus. Did he have a large following? Whose side was he on? Could a man like him, Simon, count on their support if he got cornered? How well trained were this man's followers? What kind of a fight could they put up? And he laughed as he stroked his horse's neck.

Looking up at him, I said this Galilean appeared to be only a healer, one of those messianic figures. Not a warrior. And as far as I knew, the Romans as yet didn't take him as a serious threat. Anyway, I wasn't much interested in the Galilean.

Watching him ride away, I knew that a word passed on from him to the Romans would have me crucified. Yet it didn't seem to matter; he fascinated me with his own wild world of wonder. The Jews believed they were unlike all other peoples, but Simon went further; he was even unlike the rest of the Jews.

I kept on meeting him and passing on information about the departure of rich caravans, the roads they would follow, the hour of departure — and soon Simon became so famous I heard Roman soldiers talking about him. At first I did not notice that doing these things was bringing a change in me, a change in little things, just little things. I used to ask Mary if she had heard from Judas, but now I noticed that if she had told me he was near, I would have avoided him, believing he could learn at a glance things about me he shouldn't know, and would then look down on me.

V

It is the little things, the unexpected little things, that shame a man. I would be sitting in the tavern near the Antonia, the one used so much by the Romans, and soldiers joking and laughing, cursing and singing, would see me come in, and would say hello to me with friendly respect. Then a grin on one young face, the brown eyes meeting mine, seeming to hold mine a little long, would give me a pang as if I knew this one was to die in some ambush in the hills. Or a little thing like a visit with Marcellus to the games, when he would be sitting beside me, and as he leaned back, his arm would come around my shoulder, and he would talk on in such utter ease with me, he didn't even have to turn to see if I listened. Or I might be thinking of Pilate coming back soon to Jerusalem with the troops, and there would pop into my head the face of Pilate's beautiful wife, the blue eyes on me, the blue eyes full of strange, wise, gentle understanding. Well, I learned to protect myself against these unexpected little things. As soon as they touched me, bringing that dreadful sense of humiliation, I would think of the growing pile of silver, my share of Simon's booty, hidden in my room. Simon would sell the stuff for silver, and in my mind I counted the money. I kept counting and weighing and counting again till there was nothing in my mind but silver figures, and as I added them I got excited.

Then came the time when Mary journeyed to Samaria to see her family. She had begged me to go with her because she was going in style with fine rich clothes I had given her, and with a dream the clothes seemed to bring closer to her, the dream of soon being with me in Rome; and she could tell this to her mother. Though I knew she wanted to show me off to her family, I could not go with her. I had too much work to do. I rode out with her as far as the inn that is just up the highway from the West Gate. It was the week of the dry spell. It was hot in its own Judean way, for the sun here is like no other sun around the great sea. It comes straight at you, straight, hard, and cruel, and into this hot dryness came little gusts of wind from the desert.

When the caravan stopped at the inn, Mary got out of the cart so we could have a minute by ourselves walking arm in arm on the footpath by the great highway, the traffic streaming by; farmers with carts of produce, peasants driving little herds of goats, horsemen dismounting for drink at the inn before entering the city, occasionally a few Roman soldiers escorting some special foreign merchant. At the inn's door stood that lean, leathery-faced bald innkeeper watching me, recognizing me, I was sure, since I had so often met Simon here. After helping Mary up to her cart seat, I mounted my horse. Then she turned, her hand going to her mouth, the brilliant sunlight on her coppery hair. But the happiness I saw in her smile suddenly became a shaming thing, for I knew I could not take her to Rome. Even if I heard from the senator that the coast was clear, I could not leave Judea, bound as I was to Simon; and hurting, I reached for the picture of the pile of silver, the mental arithmetic, counting and counting, trying to believe as I counted that if a man had enough money, if the pile would keep growing . . .

That night, after quickly falling into a deep sleep, I had a nightmare that made me jump up in bed and watch the faces of my mother and father float around the room as they searched for me, and I tried to cry out, "Here I am," but words wouldn't come out. I was choking. Thrashing around, I woke up. In a cold sweat I got up and sat in the dark on the edge of the bed, listening to the beating of my heart, and I could hear Simon, standing by the campfire in the hills, say, "I know I'm right about you."

Burning with humiliation, I had to get up. Stumbling around the room in the dark, I told myself I was a miserable traitor. Information coming from me had led to good men being ambushed and killed. I had betrayed the friendship of Marcellus and the good will of Pilate and the men I worked with; if they knew about me they would gladly have watched me being skinned alive. And yet I had done these things so easily, and, shaken, I wondered if I had lost all sense of myself. Then I remembered my father talking to me the day I left Crete to take up service in Rome: "And remember this, if you really want to get to know a man, find out things he will not do." And I felt lonely and afraid.

But when at last it was broad daylight I found my terrors vanishing. I slept. By midday I could tell myself the things of the night are always killed off by a good sound sleep.

I went to the marketplace as usual, keeping an eye out for Simon. But not until he tugged at my sleeve did I recognize him. He wore a handsome turban of gold cloth he had taken from some merchant, and a fine long black silk coat from some other traveller. I had been looking for a shabby farmer. "Is this you, O great prince?" I asked, feeling the warmth in him for me, and as soon as I began passing on some information about caravans leaving in the morning I got that tingle of nervous excitement that I seemed to need.

While we talked, people came streaming past us from the marketplace heading east. Over there a parade was coming down the street. I love a parade, and so we followed the crowd to see whose parade it was. If Simon had looked like a shabby farmer, as he often did, I would have been conspicuous walking with him, and we would have parted quickly. Now he was dressed as well as I was. He limped along beside me. The limp justified the long heavy cudgel he carried.

The wind had changed, there was now a stench in the air. "I can't get used to it," I said, looking up at the temple on the hill. The secret of the tribal power hidden there in those stones. Was it the only thing they believed in — their tribal power hidden in stone? I said, "Simon, is there a thirst for blood here in that stench? What do you think?" We were in a line of people and Simon, forgetting to limp, walked upright like a strong man. "It's interesting, Philo," he said. "The whole mystery of the Jewish faith is in this belief in life. Yet, they keep the blood flowing, eh? Oh, they really do."

And I said, "Not Jewish blood, Simon. Maybe their

God has reverence only for Jewish life." Then I dug my elbow into him, pointing at his foot. He was not limping, and three old white-bearded men near by had noticed his sudden firm stride. Resuming his limp, he said, "Where do you keep your gods, Philo?"

And just as we got to the street along which the parade was coming and found a place against the wall of a house where we could watch, I told him the gods might be in caves or in the sky. The Phoenicians said they lived in trees, and I told him I had friends in Herculaneum who say the Egyptian Isis is there right now. But it was my view that since the gods act through us, they must be in our own heads, which was why we seem to wear them out, and they have to change their names to keep alive — and so even my Aphrodite, who had her temple and statue in Crete, may have to change her name so she can go on watching over mariners at sea and cities near the sea.

"It's all right with me," Simon said. "Look, whose parade is this? Which one this time?"

It was a strangely quiet crowd. If it had been a patriotic parade there would have been shouting and cheering. These marchers were women and men and they weren't really marching. They straggled along, some two hundred of them, surging back and forth around a mounted man whose face I could not see for he kept turning, raising his hand and turning. I was as baffled by the antics of the marchers as Simon was. We looked at each other, shrugging in wonder. These bearded old men, these boys, these farmers, these cripples, a few good-looking young women and a hundred others who looked like beggars, would turn to shout at the mounted young man. "He is king. He is king," they cried, their own faces shining with happiness. The younger men were dancing around a little. Old men, throwing out their arms exultantly, beckoned to the silent spectators to come and share the triumph, for to these motley marchers it was a triumph. One old man passing near me wept, and the boy who held his hand had the heavens in his eyes. I heard singing. I saw a beautiful woman in a blue robe walking near the mounted man. I liked the way she walked. The man wore a white cloak and I tried to see his face as he passed, but he had bent down to speak to the woman. I heard her laugh, and when she laughed like this I thought they were all going to break into a dance, and go dancing down the street.

As a stout woman, watching, lurched against Simon, he said to her, "What is this rabble?"

"The Galilean," she said. "His followers."

"The Galilean," Simon said to me. "Imagine," and he laughed in disgust. "So this is the one I've heard about. I've heard about the big crowds he draws. I've wanted to meet him. I thought the time might come when I might need him to hide me or protect me. But look at his crowd. You'd have to sweep the taverns and the jails to get such a lot. Ten of my men could chase them."

"Simon, he's a mounted man."

"So he is. So what?"

"Any mounted man who leads a parade into a city has to be watched, Simon — if the poor, in thousands, are behind him. The Romans know this — see there, see those soldiers."

Then I broke off; I saw Judas. Well back in the parade, he wore a yellow cloak, richly yellow, and this time without the blue adornment, and he had on a fine yellow turban he must have picked up in some other land. He walked as if he knew he did not have to be among the group of men keeping close to the leader. Those near him, the mounted man, those all around him, had a kind of euphoric air, all being in the grip of some sort of triumph, but Judas, with his serene expression, looked like a prince who had travelled in many lands, and all that he had learned in Athens or Egypt or Persia had worn off on him, and he knew he was exactly where he wanted to be, and his master knew this too.

As he passed just ten feet away he saw me. His face lit up and he called, "Philo." I waved, but as he was carried along he beckoned, pointing ahead, beckoning and pointing in the direction the parade was going, and I knew he wanted me to follow along, maybe even as far as the Mount of Olives.

"Who's that man?" Simon asked.

"His name is Judas," I said.

"Is he rich?"

"I don't know. I don't think so. I don't know. Why?"

"He doesn't look as if he ever needed money."

"It's a noble air, Simon."

"He's a proud man, Philo. So what is he doing with this crowd? Where does he come from?"

Spectators were now falling behind the parade, some continuing to follow even as it turned toward the hill, others like us heading back to the marketplace, and Judas was in my mind, upsetting me, and I wanted to get him out of my head, so I quickly told Simon how I had met him. Then I became aware that Simon limping along, still very much the elegant prince, was eyeing me, wondering why I was troubled.

Heavy clouds had suddenly closed over the sun and a wind came up — for the first time in days, a wind, and bits of market refuse were blown toward us across the cobblestones, and I said, "Simon. I can't go on with this."

"This story about Judas?"

"No, listen, please, Simon," I said desperately. "I know I made a bargain with you. You gave me my life for what I offered, and Simon — hear this — the bargain became easier because I loved being with you. But now I can't sleep at night. I work with men — I'm one of them. I have no life of my own, Simon. I can't go on."

"You would break with me?"

"Not with you. With what I do."

"I see," he said, peering at me. Then his silence began to crush me, and I cried, "Simon, I've told you."

"Yes," he said slowly, "and I thought you were so much at ease with me, always at ease."

"I like being with you."

"But you want to stop?"

"I have to stop."

"No matter what happens to you?"

"I have to stop, Simon."

Without answering, he squatted down on the cobblestones there near the crowded marketplace. Cross-legged, he sat in silence in his great turban and fine black silk coat staring at the tiers of stone houses on the hill, maybe staring beyond at the cloudy sky, the clouds racing in the growing wind. And suddenly in my nervousness and fear of his silence as he turned in so deeply on himself, I wished it were nighttime and he was squatting in the hills, reading the stars, where he could find his real, ancient wisdom about people.

I began to circle around him saying unrelated things. I said I knew I was at his mercy. I could not run. I knew he could have some blind man or beggar pass on the word about me and I would surely die, and what was most terrible for me was that I loved him for being what he was. A few drops of rain fell. He stood up, and in a moment of majestic silence, his eyes met mine, and he said quietly, "You are right. You are what you are, a scholar. I am what I am. I trust you. We like each other. You should be free of me. You are now, Philo."

"Nothing more from me?"

"Nothing. Except your friendship."

"Any time, Simon. I'll look for you."

"In Rome, too, you'll look for me?"

"In Rome, too, Simon."

"Remember this, Philo," he said, his left hand on my shoulder and his right hand in mine. "What I know about you, what you have done for me here in Jerusalem, is hidden forever. So feel free, Philo. I would never betray you."

He was limping away from me, big-shouldered, pounding his cudgel on the stones. He didn't look back and I watched him, full of vast surprise, and relief. It had come so easily, like a grace from him — a great wild thief full of grace — and I could hardly believe it. A gust of wind blew dust and sand around his feet. A frisky black dog, coming out of nowhere, trotted after him.

Only when he was hidden among carts and merchants could I move. A girl, tugging at my sleeve, wanted to tell my fortune. She was full of wild fantasies that took in everything she thought I wanted to hear, and I gave her a coin, laughing; then I wanted to get home. I felt light and exhilarated. I couldn't go up to the Mount of Olives and see Judas. I wanted to see him now, but I had to get my work done so I could go tomorrow to Mary, who would be back from Samaria. I could sleep tonight. At last I could have a good sleep. What the whole world needed was a good sleep.

It started to rain again, but just a little light shower. Then sudden sunlight made the wet air sparkle.

VI

As soon as she came to the door I remembered how she looked crouched naked on the bed, long coppery hair falling over one breast, eyes searching mine and making me feel I was there, but yet not there, one of many men — and yet that's not accurate at all, and I don't know why it comes to mind. At the door I knew something was wrong as soon as she said she'd walk down the road and tell me where she had been. It was my own house and she was keeping me out. Brushing past, I asked, "Where is he?" I remember the long silence and how she sat there. "What happened in Samaria?" I asked. Smiling, she whispered, "I never got to Samaria." Then I got hold of myself and sat down and said, "So you never got to Samaria. Then where have you been?"

She told me the little caravan going along the highway had come to a crossroad where a crowd had gathered, listening to a speaker. They had got off the wagon to stretch their legs. And while she listened to the young man telling a story, Judas, who was among those who were close to the storyteller, recognized her. He came over and took her closer, and when the storyteller smiled at her, maybe because she was listening so raptly, Judas asked if she would like to meet him.

"Judas?" I said.

"Yes, Judas," she said. Judas took her by the hand and led her to the storyteller, and when he put out his hand and touched her she was full of wonder because she knew she could not leave; and the caravan went on its way without her. "And he seemed to know I was a harlot, but he made me feel it didn't matter now — I was held in wonder." In her sudden silence as she nursed her wonder, she had a new mysterious sensuality for me and I felt pain. "I fell at his feet, kissing his feet, feeling my life had been so ugly, and the storyteller, touching my head said, 'Now you're really beautiful.'"

"Judas," I said bitterly. "Judas led you to him."

"Yes."

"Judas knew you were my girl. He brought you to me."

"I know he did, Philo."

"Do you work for Judas?"

"Work?"

"Has he other girls like you?"

"Oh, Philo."

"I'm not a fool. Don't you be such a fool," I said angrily. "That man Judas sees his master looking at you and smiling, and so he takes you by the hand — his little offering to the master. It didn't matter that he had brought you to me. And I liked him. I looked up to him. Oh, the favor-currying son of a pig! I looked up to him and he sold me out," and the sound of my own words gave me pain, and when she said almost affectionately,

"It wasn't like that at all, Philo," the pain in me deepened. "I know I'm a harlot, Philo," she said. "You knew it when Judas brought me to you."

"You're not a harlot to me," I said. "Never mind what you are to Judas," and trembling I took her hand and kissed it reverently. Just a few feet away was the door of the little room with the silken couch where she had often lain naked, the oil lamp throwing golden patches on her marvellous breasts as her baffling little laugh came out of the shadows. As I glanced at this room, I remembered how as we rested she would snuggle against me, and we would talk about Rome and how she would always be in my life.

I got myself a cup of wine, and one for her too, from the little table. And as I handed her the wine and she sipped it, I said gently, "You say you looked at that man and he made you feel your life had been ugly up to now. But it's not true, Mary." Then I told her anything beautiful was good, and as for there being anything ugly about her, well, to the end of my days I would remember that when I had the fever and wanted to die she comforted me with her warm flesh and made me want to live and love and if this wasn't beautiful, then people could find no beauty in each other or in the warm glory of the senses. And remember this, I said, all those crazy kings in the hills were good at casting spells and gathering disappointed women around them. Hadn't she noticed?

I upset her a little. As she sipped her wine I saw her eyes over the rim of her glass. Something bothered her. Then she shrugged. All the women weren't drab and disappointed, she said. I should meet Mary Magdalene. "He kisses her," she said. "He kisses her publicly, he kisses her on the mouth," and I said nothing. In the long

silence I felt her wondering about these things. I felt it
with satisfaction and I said, "I must have seen her in his
parade — the one very close to him. Very pretty, too."

"Yes."

"Not your hair, though. Not your beautiful hair."

"Hers is black — long and black."

"Is she one of Judas's ladies?"

"Stop it, Philo."

"Doesn't she know Judas well? Very well?"

"Everybody knows Judas. What is this, Philo?" and
then shaking her head, frowning, she said, "I know I
can't have him all to myself, but it doesn't matter. I know
that that shiver of ecstasy that comes in my body when
I'm really making love with you is just a taste, a promise
of what can come that is nothing to do with my body.
Look, Philo, I know I'm not a scholar like you. I'm ignor-
ant, but I've been proud, and knew there was no shame
in being a harlot. But when he said, 'Now you're really
beautiful —' it was his voice — no, not just his voice, it
was all around me — the whole world there as I had
never seen it before, and I was more beautiful than I had
ever been. I was, Philo — it was as if a lovely flower was
growing in me . . ."

The break in her voice, the expectancy in her face,
upset me. I could see that this Galilean could have the
power of casting spells, turning fantasies into spells, and
then I felt a wrench at my whole being as if things were
being torn from me. And yet I tried to laugh.

"How do they do it?" I said. "How do they get away
with it? Is he going to look after you, Mary?"

"I'll be looked after."

"What about your mother and your little sisters when
they get hungry?"

"I don't know."

"Don't you care? Or will Judas look after them?"

"I don't know."

"They're all poor, this crowd, and I know you, Mary. Well, what has he promised you?"

"A whole kingdom, Philo."

"Really?" and I laughed. "Where's yours to be, Mary?"

"Within me," she said softly.

"Within you?"

"That's what he said."

"Within you," I repeated, still astonished. "These fantasies, oh, these Jewish fantasies," I said. "Well, you're in with a strange crowd, Mary. They'll take everything from you. They'll take everything. These men in the hills are all thieves. Simon, the Idumaean, takes with the sword. He empties purses, he takes anything he can sell. This Galilean empties hearts with his spells — don't you see, Mary?"

Circling around her, making her follow me with her eyes, I joked about her Galilean. What was the man up to? I had seen his parade, his big parade, I said, and I laughed again. A comic parade, a real circus of sick old men, thieves, beggars, harlots, and farmers who threw palm leaves in his path, crying out he was king, though anyone could see they'd all run like rabbits at the first blast of a horn. And I kept on because she was nodding, apparently impressed. Then, keeping a straight face, she clapped her hands, slow heavy clapping in mocking applause.

It stung me. I grabbed her, and kept her hard against me, excited by her blazing eyes, her coppery hair swinging on her golden dress. As she clawed at me, she tore at my hair like an animal, just as she used to do in one of her tantrums. I was delighted, and laughed as if I knew of old we now were for each other, and I picked her up, her legs kicking, and carried her into the bed where she lay panting, her eyes closed, and there I pulled the dress from her shoulders and caressed her lovely breasts.

I kissed the nipples. She didn't move. I caressed her belly and she didn't move, and then I was gentle with my touch between her legs, gentle and waiting, but she remained utterly inert, her eyes still closed, dead to me now no matter what I did, and I got up slowly, burning with humiliation. Nothing was said. I got out.

My horse was stabled at the inn, down the road a little way, because I had expected to stay the night with Mary. I started down the highway. A wind was coming up and I ducked my head against the dust-laden gust. It was going to rain, the wind was heavy with rain. Carts and donkeys and men on horseback came hurrying by me, trying to get into Jerusalem before the rain. Dust unlike the dust on a road in any other country, gritty heavy desert dust, bit at my face as I thought about the Galilean. I couldn't concentrate on him. I didn't know him. There was only one thing I knew. I was sure he would have reminded Mary he was Jewish, and she was too, and I wasn't. Then I told myself that a sensual holy man was a new reference for Mary — a novelty — all the charm of novelty, but this charm could not last, and in this way I got by the Galilean in my thoughts.

I got to Judas. I couldn't understand how he could have been so concerned, trying to look after me in my sickness. There had been nothing in it for him. He had asked for nothing, and how did it happen that I had come to look up to him, seeing him in a mysterious light, a man from many lands who knew things others could not know? Had he built himself up? Or had he let me do it? I wondered. My own Judas! I created my own Judas out of the strong impression he had made on me. Yet why had he bothered with me? Unless he liked manipulating people. Unless he saw himself always in a certain high light. Maybe with Mary he was trying now to manipulate his leader. So why should I count? Why shouldn't the dog sell me out? I asked these questions and kept asking them because deeper within me, bothering me, was an intimation that my life was about to take another turn.

Then the rain came. It soaked me, and the dusk got darker. And in that light the great shadow of the turreted Jerusalem wall hung over me.

VII

Then there was another parade in Jerusalem. Pilate had entered the city. He paraded his troops through the streets so that those lower priests who hated the Sanhedrin's collaboration with the Romans and would like to use the great festival to stir up hostility could see how many troops were in the city now. For days the great highways had been crowded. Thousands and thousands had come trudging in from the hills and the villages, bringing with them animals that were to be slaughtered at the temple. Everyone was now looking for a good time.

I was too busy to get out much. The garrison commander kept me busy preparing reports for Pilate. The work was good for me, since it took my mind off Judas and Mary and the Galilean, and when I could get out I found the city's carnival atmosphere exhilarating. As I wandered around I kept an eye open for Simon who, I was sure, would be wearing one of his ridiculous disguises. All the narrow streets and all the little houses were jammed with people who drank, danced, quarrelled and feasted and littered the streets, the whole scene a delight to my senses.

But the temple was a great slaughterhouse, stinking of blood, though water from the spring under the temple cleaned the sacred stone and carried the blood away, and all the animals, waiting, cooped up in the courts, stank too. Blood, blood, sacrificial blood, as I had said to Simon, the smell always in the air, while happy people in a gay restless mood after sacrificing jumped around in joy, looking for unexpected adventure. The farmers and their wives and children mingled with city folk, all wearing their best clothes and bright-colored turbans. As they danced around in the streets, the turbans looked like wind-blown flowers in golden sunlight; behind them was the green mountain, all of it now a great garden, and hundreds of people, linking arms in a great chain and singing an ancient song with a haunting rhythmic beat, danced forward, kicking, then back, kicking in a beautiful pattern of blazing color as those watching cried out in tribal joy. It was such a sight I wished I were a painter painting in that sunlight and catching the flesh tones and the colored turbans in their sunlit patterns.

Then one night when I was looking for Simon in the crowded smelly streets, the walls seemed to close in on me till the narrow street was an open window on the night sky; the sky a sea, the street a narrow window on the sea. The great sea! Not the desert. The Jews knew nothing about the great sea — just the desert. And there that night on the narrow street I did a little reflecting; I told myself I mustn't be a fool. I didn't care about the Galilean and no one was going to get me involved with him, and besides, I had heard from Lepidus, the garrison commander, that the Galilean had drawn a great crowd in the countryside and was hated by the priests, who had seen him come into the city at the head of a parade. My main concern now was to remain free of any involvement that would keep me in Jerusalem after I heard from the senator, who by this time ought to have been able to work the magic of his money and influence. Now might be the time to write to him.

But then the next day Pilate's wife asked for me, and when I went to her apartment she told me she wanted me to take down a long letter to her sister in Rome. I had often done these letters to the sister. I liked doing them not only because Pilate's wife was such a lovely woman — although there might be greater beauties right here in Jerusalem — but because she had a luminous quality that enchanted me. I was aware of her sexuality too, also enchanting, a secret thing with her. In Pilate's court in Caesarea many of the ladies shared in the general debauchery around them. Because the place was so provincial these ladies often did strange things to stimulate their sexual appetites. But not Pilate's wife. She didn't need to. Her sensuality, this secret thing, was in every little movement of her arm, or her glance at her own ankle.

And I liked working for her because she was such a natural storyteller. This time while I was scribbling away, wondering at the mystery of her narrative ease, I realized that she was telling stories about the Galilean. She was talking about miracles, the dead rising, the blind seeing. As I looked up in astonishment, she said, "What is it, Philo?"

"I didn't quite hear," I said, ducking my head and trying to scribble rapidly to hide my astonishment. She wasn't a little Jewish girl in a village, or a farmer in the hills, or a fisherman living on fantasies and encouraging them in others. She was a civilized Roman! She went on dictating. "I dreamt about the Galilean last night." The baffled expression on my face made her smile. "Are you not interested in these wonders, Philo?" she asked. I said, "Madam, this is a land of wonders." But I couldn't imagine how the Galilean had reached her. Without even meeting her, he had had the magic to get into her dreams.

After I left her I hurried through my other work. Then, late in the afternoon, I headed for Ezekiel's house, where I had to wait to see him. He had a patient, a rich woman with a young daughter with no breasts, and the mother, grieving for the daughter, kept bringing her to Ezekiel, who had been giving the girl a potion. I watched them leaving. After talking to Ezekiel the slim girl had a misty-eyed hopeful expression on her pretty face. She glowed when Ezekiel kissed her forehead almost reverently, and Ezekiel looked as ungainly and sloppy as ever, in spite of the fine new robe I had picked out for him at his tailor's.

When he had got some wine I told him I had heard so many stories about the Galilean and his power over big crowds that I was fascinated, and since he was there on the Mount of Olives, I wondered if we could go together and listen to him preach and find out what the man was up to.

Surprised, he said, "Haven't you heard, Philo?"

"Heard what?"

"The man has been arrested."

"Arrested? When was this?"

"Last night."

"Why was he arrested? Who arrested him?"

"Well," Ezekiel began, smiling, "it seems the man really believes he is the Son of God. What do you do? So the council condemned him. Blasphemy, Philo. He's charged with blasphemy. And this you won't like, Philo," he said with a certain satisfaction. "It seems that one of his own men betrayed him. Guess who?"

"Who?"

"That friend of yours who took charge when you had the fever — Judas. He led the guard to him and pointed him out."

"Judas?"

"Judas."

"Why? Do they know why?"

"Money. They say quite a bit of money changed hands. Are you really stunned, Philo?"

"So he sold him out," I said softly, and I wanted to add, "Sold him out, too," but catching myself, I was silent, nursing a sardonic satisfaction.

"You're smiling to yourself," Ezekiel said.

"I am?"

"I didn't like him. But I thought you'd be shocked."

"No. You were right about him, Ezekiel. Nothing gets in his way. The Galilean must have been in the way. To what? What's he up to, I wonder."

But something about the story was nagging away at me. "You said he led the guard to him?" I asked.

"So they said."

"And was paid to do this."

"Exactly, Philo."

"Surely you got it wrong, Ezekiel. Nobody had to lead the guard to the Galilean's place and point him out. Everybody in the city knew where he was. And everybody knew the Galilean, and what he looked like. No one had to point him out. He wasn't in hiding, was he? No one had to be led to the hiding place." I don't know why I grew uneasy. "What's going on around here, Ezekiel?"

"What do you mean?"

"Surely you can see the story doesn't make any sense?"

"Well, yes," he said after pondering for a minute. "Maybe I got it wrong, Philo. Maybe this Judas is the one who accused Jesus of blasphemy, maybe he has agreed to appear before the council and denounce him. That must be it."

"At least it makes more sense," I said. "Where's he being held?"

"At the high priest's house."

"No Romans in on this at all?"

"It's a civil matter, a religious matter. As you know, Philo. They get involved only if he is to be executed."

"At the priest's house, eh? What about his followers? Lepidus tells me he has thousands and thousands. Won't they now be at the priest's house to take him? Won't there be rioting, Ezekiel?" And I thought of Mary; carried away as she was, she would be there with the others, wailing and ranting and rushing at the house. I could see her struck down. I tensed at the thought. Ezekiel said, "Why let it bother you? Look, I'll try and find out the facts about your friend Judas." I nodded and tried to laugh. But I finished my drink and left him.

The priest's house was in the lower city, a very long walk away. But the stables of the Antonia were not far off, and there I got a horse. Just as I was mounting, Marcus, the second in command, saw me as he left the stables. He was in a jovial mood for such a bitter man, and asked me to go with him to the tavern for a drink. I told him I couldn't, I didn't have the time. Grinning up at me, slapping my leg, he said, "By the way, Philo, we caught a brigand, a fine fat brigand, and brought him here in chains. Simon, the Idumaean. Ever hear of him?" Stiff in the saddle, I waited, then felt such a wrench at my heart that I couldn't move. Then I think I grinned down at Marcus, and slapped the horse again to have him gallop as if now it was really necessary to get to the high priest's house quickly. When the horse stumbled on the cobblestones, I held him in, trembling, and in a slow trot we went down the hill and into the demon-infested valley.

As the even drumming of the horse's hooves on the stones began to jar at my skull, the terrible truth struck me. Simon could have been riding with me, pleading with me for understanding. Wouldn't any man try and bargain for his life, particularly if he had a young wife he loved? He wouldn't *want* to betray me. He liked me, he trusted me, I knew he did, but as the hours shortened for him, how could he hold on to his loyalty to me with a voice within him whispering, "I must live, I must live."

Yes, Simon would suffer more for betraying me, knowing my affection for him. In his heart he would be begging me to forgive him for bargaining for his life. And he would want to talk to me gently, so that he could bring me to accept the necessity of his betrayal.

In the valley, with people on the street, I had been walking the horse. I had to stop to let a group of singing children pass. I looked down at their faces. A yapping dog came frisking around the horse's legs, moving us on, and we nearly knocked over a big-eyed little girl who wouldn't move. As we moved on up the hill I remembered Simon sitting cross-legged in the marketplace, silly in his fine silk merchant's coat, then rising, a smile on his big bearded face, as he said quietly, "I would never betray you, Philo."

As I got closer to the high priest's house I expected to hear shouting or screaming or even singing, all the sounds of an angry crowd, but I heard no cries, and when I came to the house no one was there, not even a little group weeping and wailing, not one man beating his head on the ground, crying out for the release of the master. What's going on, I wondered.

It was late afternoon and the house was in strong sunlight when into the light came four men carrying a handsome litter. At the house a brilliant apparition appeared. It startled me. Stiff in the saddle, I stared and stared, full of wonder, dazzled by the majesty and power of this apparition from another, barbaric world. On his head was a tiara and under it a beautiful turban with a gold plate with the god's name inscribed on it. Golden bells encircled his ankle-length robe and when he moved the tinkling bells seemed to be calling, gently calling those demons that came at night to the valley, urging them to leave him alone. On his breast was the god's oracle, which was set with twelve precious gems for the different tribes, all gold-linked; and a mantle of beautiful embroidered flowers, glittering with gems of many hues, all blazing in the sun, wrapped him in a rainbow glow that made him look as if he had dropped in on the earth from the stars and brought all his nocturnal powers with him.

Then I realized it was Caiaphas, the high priest — Caiaphas, whom I knew to speak to, but had never seen in his full regalia, in his real magic light. And I was shaken. I saw now in him the secret of his people. It was hidden in some of them, yet in them all just the same. They were all from this other world — Mary, Judas, the Galilean locked in that house, and Simon, too — and in their secret security they didn't really care what I thought or felt, or how anyone judged them. So I could never really know them. I couldn't know Simon. I couldn't know what he would say or do or think, now that his life was at stake.

Then Caiaphas, after looking searchingly at me, a lone horseman watching him, got on the litter and was carried away. The last of the strong sunlight shone on the terraced hills, and the stone city again looked like a giant yellow desert flower.

VIII

In the great Antonia fortress was the prison, and the prison walls had little slits for windows, and from one of these slits you could see the great courtyard, then the stables. Soldiers were always in the courtyard, standing around in groups, or forming patrols, taking instructions, or coming with horses from the stables. Outside the fortress walls were the streets, which could also be seen from the prison because the neighborhood was on the downward slope of the great hill. It was a very small Roman neighborhood with three taverns and many little Jewish shops. In the evenings soldiers loafed along the streets with their girls. There were always enough girls, and they sang and drank with the soldiers in the taverns.

When I reached the courtyard I stared up at those slits in the prison wall. Simon could be watching the figures moving in the courtyard, and I was sure he could have picked me out. By this time I could feel his eyes on me; it was a terrible thing that he was so close at hand, and I was sure that under the torture he had cried out that he had information. If the cry stopped the torture it could also save his life. My eyes on the prison wall, I told myself there was no reason why Simon should suffer and die for me. Why me? How could he care about me? I had nothing he needed, nothing to love, so what was I to him? I couldn't even believe I had ever even amused him very much. I had no recollection of him roaring with laughter. There was just this: my heart ached that he should be lying in chains so near to me. As I hurried away, his great, wild, bearded face seemed to be right beside me, and I could hear him say, "You forget, Philo, I'm still a proud, defiant man."

By nightfall, in spite of this strange primitive faith in Simon that was underneath all my fears, I became so apprehensive about his nearness that I had to get away from the fortress. I imagined that all the passing Romans were looking at me with curiosity. Word must have got around. I was waiting to be seized. I went home.

Yet there, too, I waited for the pounding on the door. Finally I unlocked the door and left it wide open, so no one could say I had barred the way. Then I sat down to concentrate on a plan. If only Simon had been one of those messiah brigands from the countryside, there would be a crowd now outside the prison wall, all wailing and screeching and crying out to the god of Israel to release him. If only — if only. But no one was there at the wall. Just as there had been no one outside the high priest's house where the Galilean was imprisoned. The only thing that could save Simon, after a death sentence, I thought, was an intervention. But only Pilate could intervene. No one else, no one! I concentrated and concentrated, and from the streets came the sound of footsteps, then the sound of a lazy, sensual woman's laugh, the same laugh I might have heard in Alexandria or Rome. It got dark, but I stayed there on the bed. I could think better in the dark. Finally I got up, washed myself, and went to Ezekiel's house.

It was one of Ezekiel's evenings of music, fine food, wine, and amusing conversation. People could drop in. When I arrived, the portly aristocrat Ananaus and his pretty young wife were there and Mordechai, the scholar with the elegant hands, who played the harp like a master, and whose beautiful wife from Tyre sometimes sang with him while he played, and there were two intellectual priests, Phineas and Eleazar. After two cups of wine I became talkative and jovial, and as witty as I could be. It was necessary that they pay attention to me and listen. So I teased Ezekiel about his liking for Greek things. I told him it was because he recognized that the Greek period in Judea had been the civilizing time in Judea, and then we got into a slanging match. Sprawled out on his big cushion, Ezekiel would hurl a devastating insult at me, just a short sentence or two, and then, showing no wound, I would insult him even more wittily, and on and on, as if we were tearing each other to pieces, while the others laughed and applauded. When we grew tired of it, we had some food and drink.

All this time music and singing were coming from the lovely garden. I didn't know who was out there. At these events there was always the music and always the pretty faces and sweet voices of those women. Then I asked idly if this Simon, the Idumaean, the bandit now in prison, wasn't some kind of a Jewish hero. "Simon, the Idumaean," the young priest Eleazar said. "We hear about him. Everybody hears about him. No one knows him."

"All he's doing," the portly Ananaus said, "is robbing the Romans and making trouble for us all." They all agreed. The young priest Eleazar, however, said, "Just the same he must be a wild, audacious man. I've heard stories of his bravery."

The rich Ananaus insisted he didn't want any trouble with Romans. The health of the Romans at present was the health of the Jews, he said, and the high priest, Caiaphas, and Pilate had an excellent collaboration. No one in his right mind wanted a threat to the peace. Never mind about Simon, he said. The Galilean, the blasphemer, was the real threat. He stirred up discontent, roused the rabble against the rich, and tried to separate the people from their priests. Hadn't they all heard him wrangling with the Pharisees in the temple court? Quick-witted and dangerous. They all agreed. Even Ezekiel.

I said with an ironic shrug, "I'm not allowed in the inner court," and was astonished at how quickly these people of such disparate views could come together, sensing a threat to their temple secret.

The young priest Eleazar, who had long curls and a beautiful voice, waited a moment, then said uneasily that no one knew where the Galilean's followers were hiding now, or what they might be planning. Why were they all hiding? When would they come out of hiding? What were they waiting for? he asked. Even outside the high priest's house where the Galilean was being detained, none of his followers had appeared, crying out his name. That was a very strange thing, wasn't it? What were they waiting for? A sign? What sign? Who was to give them this sign?

"This is all very interesting," I said, shrugging as if I were really puzzled. "I hear talk among officials and captains, and they don't care who's hiding and waiting for a sign," and I laughed. "It's not your Galilean *they're* interested in."

"No?" Ezekiel asked. "Who?"

"This Simon, the Idumaean."

"A thorn in their side?"

"More than that, Ezekiel." After pondering, I said innocently, "Isn't it strange they know so much more about Simon than you do? I've heard such stories about the man. Yes, I can't help wondering about this strangely powerful, almost mythical man, who has kept to the hills. Why does he keep to the hills?" When they pressed me to go on, I said I could only try and repeat what I had heard. I went to speak, then paused, so that they could see I was truly moved. In their intelligent faces there was wonder now. Keeping my voice down, I seemed to be trying to see Simon, a big-shouldered man, a big beard, as they said, eyes full of laughter, then blazing with defiance.

Then I said that the Romans had long been concerned about Simon because he was so unlike the other patriotic bandits. It seemed that he didn't want to head a revolt, he didn't want to come into Jerusalem as king. He was the free Jew, the eternal Jew, who couldn't bow the knee to any stranger, and in the hills the friend to any Jew in the villages or farms who wouldn't pay tribute to the stranger. Much that he took from the caravans he gave to the poor in the hills. It was Simon's ambition, according to the Roman talk, to make all roads unsafe to armed strangers. If he had his way, no Jew would ever again be at the mercy of the stranger.

The night air was full of the perfume of the heavy flowers in the garden, and the distant music and the perfume intoxicated me. Though I tried to sound casual, my imagination was getting the better of me. Every lie I told had the feel of truth for me, and I grew afraid and soon fell silent. The others, carried away by the tales I said I had heard, began to tell stories they themselves had come across. They talked with a kind of amused pride, each one exaggerating on some story. Then I broke in with a puzzled air. "I heard the captain who had taken Simon say, 'It's just as well this one has no following here, or we might soon lose him.' What did he mean, I wonder?"

"Ah, I see," Ezekiel said. "The amnesty! The Passover amnesty."

"What amnesty?" I asked, although I knew.

"It's Pilate's doing," Ezekiel said. "Pilate holds court and explains it is the custom for him to free one condemned man, one criminal about to be executed, and the crowd shouts out the name of the one they want freed."

"Now I see," I said thoughtfully. "And it could be Simon."

"It could be. If more people knew about him. If he had a political following."

I said nothing, but I got a lift, a sudden lightness within me. These men were influential. People would listen to them. I saw all the things I wanted to see now in their bright, interested faces. I drank more wine. I stayed too late. When I left the house to make my way down the hill, there was a full moon silvering the Antonia tower and the nearby temple and the street it backed on. Coming toward me were three figures, two men and a woman. The woman was in a long dark cloak, the men were dressed like farmers. One of the men limped. Earlier in the day I was sure I had seen them looking up at the window of my house. Now, as they came up the dark street, they stopped and the moonlight was on the young woman's face. It was Simon's wife. Then the heads of the men came into the same light and I recognized them: Isaiah, the son of James, and John of Jericho.

Coming closer, they waited, fearing I might choose to hurry by, simply saying, "Good night." Those two hard-faced, fiercely brutal men, who had never looked at me without cynical suspicion — well, they had changed. There was only that hard silvery streak of moonlight — but I had never seen two faces more full of trust. And Simon's wife, turned into the shadow, put out her hand and said, "Philo."

I had talked to her only once before at the inn outside the city wall a little piece down the highway — the high-waisted girl with the golden skin. The black eyes I couldn't see now. "Go. Go quickly," I said. "Not here. Don't be seen here. Are you crazy?"

"You can do something, can't you, Philo? You have such important friends."

"Before noon. Pass me in the marketplace. Just pass by. Now go."

"Philo . . ."

"Simon will not die," I said suddenly.

"He must not. . . . No."

"Simon will be free," I said and I meant it, for as her face came out of the shadow and her eyes gleamed in the moonlight, I felt buoyant with certitude after my evening's talk. Now I could see Pilate on the dais. I could hear him putting the question to the crowd. I could hear the cries: "Simon! Free Simon. Let it be Simon."

IX

And the time when Simon might be given his freedom could be close at hand, for the Sanhedrin, having had their trial of the Galilean and treated him roughly — at least so we heard at the Antonia — had condemned him to death as a blasphemer, and now they wanted to kill him. They couldn't kill him themselves. Under the law only Pilate could order an execution. Since they had brought all their documented evidence to us, supporting their charges, I was busy transcribing the documents for Pilate.

All of this had put Pilate in a bad mood; he didn't like any of it. He said so, and I was afraid to open my mouth to him, because he had made it plain long ago that he hated being drawn into cases involving Jewish religious rites and being asked to carry out the will of the Sanhedrin, or even worse, being told in effect he had to carry it out. But I wondered if he knew of that letter his wife had written to her sister, or if she had told him the Galilean had come in a dream. Anyway, he had too much self-respect to sign an execution order just because he was told to do so, and I was sure he would hold an open court. And this would be the time, indeed it had to be the time, for the gift of the amnesty.

The documents from the Sanhedrin accused the Galilean of having had himself anointed as king, of fomenting rebellion, of mocking the authority of the priests, and above all, of calling himself the Son of God, and they gave the times and the places where these things had happened, and the names of witnesses, showing how thoroughly they had kept track of him. Yet the name of Judas was not given; he wasn't named as an accuser, he wasn't named at all, and I sat back from my work table, frowning, wondering if I was caught up again in another world of wild Jewish fantasy. They were proving that they had kept track of everything the Galilean had said and done, and exactly where and when it had been said and done, and yet people were supposed to believe they had to pay money to a man named Judas to tell them where the Galilean was, and which one he was.

And this Son of God nonsense, I thought in wonder. Were they serious? The son of their Yahweh with his great thirst for sacrificial blood? Imagine! I couldn't believe they were serious. Nor could I imagine anyone else really believing it. No, there was something else, I thought, something they saw in the Galilean, a threat perhaps to the whole tribal power, and it had to be killed off.

I hurried with my work because of the appointment in the marketplace. Then I went out into the sunlight. It had been nice and cool in the Antonia with the stones always a little damp, but outside the harsh, dusty sunlight seemed to come brushing against my face. The streets were still crowded, and with Pilate's troops now in town, horsemen, little groups of them, came trotting by, and sometimes a chariot on the way to the Antonia, and all around me was such an air of bustling well-being in this real sunlit world that it seemed a terrible thing, such an offense against the whole order of nature, that I should have been fiddling with documents about a peaceful Jewish prophet who said the wrong things, when a beautiful bold man who could make my heart leap with excitement and who held my life in his hands was lying in prison awaiting his death.

When I came to the crowded marketplace and stood near the chicken coop, the squawking of the chickens filling the air, I thought I saw Simon's wife over to the right near a fruit stand. Then a stooped old man, with a bag on his shoulders, and pushing a cart and drawing two goats after him on a rope, got between us, and when the cart had passed, the woman was gone. So I wasn't sure it was Simon's wife.

Then I saw Isaiah and John coming towards me. They both had the same determined, ruthless, reckless air, and yet their faces lit up when they saw me. I had never been able to talk to these uncouth hard-eyed men; they knew I didn't like them, and yet they both grinned. They were full of friendliness, as if sure I had to have a plan; why would I be there if I hadn't made a plan? I had no plan. Suddenly their loyalty to Simon awed me. They were humble men. Isaiah had been a farmer and John a carpenter. They had nothing to believe in but their magnificent Simon.

"Have you any money? Can you get a good sum of money?" I asked, not sure what I was up to myself. I couldn't recognize my own voice.

"Simon's wife can get silver," John of Jericho said.

"How much?"

"A hundred pieces. More."

"It must be a lot more, and I'll add four hundred pieces myself. You see, my dear John," I said calmly, "everyone can be bribed if there is enough silver."

"The jailer?"

"No, the captain of the guard at the jail, a greedy man, this Anthony. A great name, I'm not sure it's his own, I've heard it's Florus. He thinks he ought to be enriching himself here in Jerusalem. He's bitter," and we talked on as if I had already had a plan afoot which I was keeping to myself. "Look for me tomorrow in this place," I said, "but if I am detained, keep looking for me. I may indeed be detained."

Leaving them, I made my way up the hill and home to have a drink with Marcellus in our tavern, and on the way I grew more and more surprised at myself. I didn't know what was driving me on so recklessly. Yet if a plan were made and it didn't work out, I thought, I would always have the hope of the amnesty to fall back on. When I got to the tavern, something prompted me to turn, and there, some thirty feet away on the street, was a young woman watching me, her figure against the sunlight: Simon's slender tall-waisted girl. How had she got here? In the marketplace, too, had she been watching, and was she to be like a shadow always behind me?

After I had the drink with Marcellus, then dinner, feeding in the warmth of his satisfaction with his love affair, I went to my own place. It was dark now. I lit the oil lamp, then looked out the window, and though it was dark, I was sure I saw someone standing on the street looking up at my window. As my stomach took a turn, I was sure Simon's wife wanted me to see her and be reminded — or warned — that Simon held my life in his hands.

Cursing, I hurried out. When she saw me coming she tried to run down the street, but I caught up, and grabbed her arm. "Listen," I said, "I told you to keep away. Soldiers are all around here. What are you trying to do? Are you threatening me?" I could hardly see her face, just the line of it in the shadow and the long neck. It's hard to describe a face you know is beautiful. The night light was on the melting eyes. In the softest voice I had ever heard, she said, "Oh, no, Philo. I only wanted you to remember that Simon would never betray you." And she fled down the street.

While I watched her vanishing down the street, I realized that while she could see the light in my window, or could see me even from a distance on the street, she had hope. I went in and sat on the bed, brooding, protesting I had never been a figure of hope in anyone's life and now I had strange mixed feelings of embarrassment and humility. Then, while I suffered, there came into my mind that time in Crete when I was only twelve years old and had been caught stealing apples from a neighbor's orchard. The neighbor came to the house complaining to my father. In the past my father had always looked down on this neighbor, and now he had to apologize profoundly. When the neighbor had gone, my father in his humiliation berated me, then punished me. I had started down the road to thievery, he said; then he sent me to bed, where I lay weeping till my mother came to me. After stroking my head she said gently, "I have the greatest faith in you, Philo. Always remember it." She was to die within the year.

As I remembered this I had another flashback in time: an evening in Rome when a dear woman friend, a centurion's wife, received news that her husband, fighting in Gaul, was missing and presumed dead. Putting my arms around her I said, "He's not dead, we'll soon hear he's not dead," and she said, "Stay near me, Philo — when you are near me I always feel so hopeful."

For a long time I went on wondering about myself, and I left the light burning all night in my window. But in the morning I was sent to Jericho with a Roman tax collector named Flavius, who was having difficulty with a Syrian merchant there and needed me as his translator. We had a fine wagon, two horses, and a driver. It was a relief to get out of Jerusalem and be some place where my thoughts could be cool and clear. This was on the day when the Galilean was sent to Pilate for an interrogation. I was glad I wouldn't be there. My nerves were too shaky, and I feared Pilate would notice I was distraught. I also imagined certain Romans would have their eyes on me, if my name had come up in the questioning of Simon.

On the Jericho journey, riding through the hills, I intended to devise a subtle approach to the captain of the prison guard. But fat old Flavius, who was becoming rich in some mysterious way, began to drive me mad with his endless talk about his crippled son who had become an important man in Rome, having a hand in the huge financial expenditures for the games. When he had exhausted the subject of his dreary son he asked if it wasn't amusing to find Pilate once again facing his Jewish dilemma. Why couldn't the procurator just let things be? he asked. Why couldn't he let the high priest have his own domain, religious and civil, and let Caiaphas condemn any one of his own people he wanted to condemn in that domain? Let him ask for a death sentence again and again. Carry it out again and again. Who cared? Why couldn't Pilate just stick to his own territory? If the high priest and his council wanted a blasphemer executed, why couldn't Pilate just do it? Who cared? Where was prudence?

"Ah, prudence, prudence," I said. "A great Greek virtue." But Pilate in his prudence hadn't bothered with Simon. Without even questioning him, he had signed the order for his execution. Now, as the wagon lurched along, the hills and valleys in sunlight and shadow kept reminding me that this was Simon's country. The hills of Simon's home, a homeland long, long before the Jews and the Canaanites, the hills where Simon may have misread the stars, or failed to read a sign at hand in the hills, not looking close enough, though the ways and the wisdom of the land were all around him and in his life, and in signs left by people in countless graves who could not take their gods with them and left them nestling in trees, or in vines, or in running streams, or in groves by forgotten gravesides, or in buried cities. Not to be warded off by tinkling bells, they still gave signs to those who had enough of the land's old wisdom to read them. And now Simon had made me part of this wisdom, counting on me.

I forget the inn where we rested the horses and ate. Nor can I remember the merchant in Jericho, who was behind in his taxes, and how Flavius dealt with him, and whether in the end there was a bribe. Nor where we ate and slept. All I can remember of Jericho is that wherever it was we stayed, I couldn't sleep, going over and over my planned approach to the prison captain, knowing how disastrous a mistake could be. In the end I was still unable to make up my mind about the right way to do it, a way that would make the bribe sound natural and inevitable. And I think it was on that night, when I was finally getting to sleep, that I woke up with a start, sure that Simon's wife, having followed me, was there by the bed.

Nor can I remember much about the journey back to Jerusalem, just that Flavius had been talking all the time, and nearing the city I heard him say, "The main thing is to avoid a riot. A big riot over the Galilean will be a nightmare this time for all of us. But you know Pilate better than I do."

"I am not his confidant," I said.

"Who is?"

"I know he's a tolerant man," I said.

"Pilate tolerant?" he said. "You should thank the gods he's not tolerant. With all the rioting going on around here, we'd all be dead if he was tolerant." And he went on to remind me that Pilate hadn't been tolerant of the Galileans when they rioted; he knew the riot would lead to an insurrection, and so he slaughtered them. A procurator's job was to carry out Roman policy, and not to be tolerant, and the policy was the same throughout the empire: no interference with the local gods, no interference with local religious customs and privileges and religious state rights — as long as the natives kept the peace and paid taxes. Another riot and slaughter could lead to a bloody insurrection in all Judea.

I knew more about the riots than Flavius. I wrote Pilate's letters. I read the letters from Rome. But Flavius droned on about his admiration of Pilate's handling of the riot over the building of the viaduct, and how he believed Pilate was right to take money from the temple treasury to build it. The treasury money, he said, was not the priests' money, it was state money, and the viaduct was to serve the state, and Pilate hadn't given in to all the screaming from the priests.

But Flavius had got me thinking of my first meeting with Pilate in Caesarea — anything to take my mind off the prison captain. Pilate knew my father-in-law, the senator, and in Caesarea when he looked at me with curiosity, I knew he was aware of my involvement in the wheat thefts. A well-built man of my height, stern-faced, with short, cropped hair and troubled blue eyes, he said nothing. He took me for what I pretended to be, a mere scribe, knowing that many Romans were in Caesarea for many different reasons. All around him was feasting, orgies, luxury, whoring, a craving for exotic self-indulgence, but he didn't care, as long as nothing was done by his officials to dishonor him and Rome. He kept out of the feasting and whoring himself because he was in love with his beautiful wife, whose eyes were as blue as his....

Then I heard Flavius say, "If Pilate could see the priest had a point about the banners, why can't he see this Galilean belongs strictly on their side of the fence, too? What do we care about a young rabbi's quarrel with the priests? It's their affair, not ours. Ask them what they want us to do, then do it, I say. Right now we're having a happy collaboration with Caiaphas. Now they love the Romans. Why spoil it? What does he care about the Galilean?"

"Maybe it's his own conscience," I said.

"Conscience," he snorted. "Conscience is what gets other people into trouble." And when he said this, I remember wondering if Pilate indeed wasn't a new man in the east, and if this wasn't why he fascinated me more and more when I wrote his letters. He wasn't an eastern tribal man. In his head, or in his heart, he had a sovereign world of his own. I have a nose for such men, but I don't find them here. But now we were entering Jerusalem, and soon I would be approaching the captain.

On my street the wet cobblestones were shining, and a young woman, holding a child by the hand, walked along, singing to herself. I knew the eyes of the first Roman I met in the Antonia would tell me whether Simon had talked. However, nothing seemed to be amiss. The gossip was all about Pilate's ingenious effort to have the Galilean taken off his hands in a way that would allow him to retain his self-respect. When the Galilean had been brought before him for questioning, Pilate had discovered he was a Galilean. Now a Galilean should be under the jurisdiction of Herod's son, and since it had come to pass that at this very time Herod's son was at the palace in Jerusalem, Pilate, maneuvering beautifully, had sent the Galilean there, asking Herod's son to deal with him.

X

The marketplace was full of arguing groups, each speaker shouting for attention. While people moved from group to group, the excitement mounted, for word had got around that Pilate, disregarding the request of the Sanhedrin that he deal summarily with the Galilean, had taken him out of the Sanhedrin's authority, and turned him over to Herod's son. Many priests were here, arguing. No doubt they were the ones who had spread the word that their established authority was being overthrown. In all the shouting I searched for Isaiah and John, the angry cries breaking into my thoughts; "Take away the power over blasphemers and you break the back of Israel." The wrangling, the vehemence, the sharp cries got on my nerves. Again this Galilean, whom I did not know, was all around me.

Then I saw Isaiah and John pushing their way towards me. "Where were you?" I said irritably as we shoved through to the outskirts.

Trying to give the impression we were watching and

listening to the speakers, we talked about money. They had got together two hundred pieces of silver; Simon's wife could find more, but it was hidden in the countryside. More time would be needed. I had four hundred pieces at my own place. Then I confessed I had no evidence that this money could help us. Could they give me this evening to see what I could do? We agreed to meet in the outer court of the temple in the morning just before noon.

At this hour of the afternoon the captain usually drank in a little place just beyond the courtyard of the Antonia. I was there sitting by myself drinking wine. Four Roman soldiers at the other end of the tavern were singing a bawdy song and roaring with laughter. I listened to many songs, I drank a lot of wine before Anthony came in and accepted my invitation to sit with me. A big florid-faced man with short graying hair, he had the disappointed eyes of so many of the Romans in Jerusalem. He had expected to prosper in this province so far from home, but among the Jews he had been given few chances to practice extortion; yet he had the air of a man who knew lush corruption was all around him. He disliked the Jews. They had disappointed him. A stingy man, he had always let me pay for his drink or his food.

We drank and gossiped; then, taking on a troubled air, I told him I had had a strange experience that should be reported. "Is this Simon, the Idumaean, a big man? Is he important?" I asked. "Or is he just another bandit?" My troubled air worked on him. "Why do you ask?" he said. I told him I had been approached near the West Gate by a poorly dressed man I thought was a beggar. But he was no beggar. Far from it. Not with his eyes, hands, and shoulders. And he knew who I was, and he said there were eight hundred pieces of silver for the man who could deliver Simon, the Idumaean, to him. Four hundred now, and four hundred when the Idumaean was free and beyond the gate. He said he felt safe, speaking to me, because I was not an official or a soldier. I was shocked — me of all people! I had put the incident out of my mind, but it kept coming back, troubling me, and now I had to report it. Did he think the man should be identified and seized? Was I doing the right thing?

"You do the right thing, Philo," he said, and then after pondering, he repeated, "Yes, you do the right thing," as if he had forgotten he had just used those words, and I waited while he remained in a trance. Then there was a sudden brightening of his eyes, and he said almost to himself, "You'd wonder how these people could have that much money, wouldn't you? It's a lot of money. It's a lot to have right in your hand, isn't it, Philo? Right in your hand, eh? These thieves must be able to save their money." Then directly to me, "Eight hundred, eh? Well, Philo, I must think about what we should do. We'll handle it. Better say nothing about this till you hear from me."

It was time for him to have his evening with his woman, and I walked down the street with him; then we stood, our heads down, holding a long silence, as if we were reluctant to part. Yes, it was a beautiful parting; we were like two dear old friends needing the moments of silent communion before we could drag ourselves away from each other.

I went to my own place and lay down, waiting, but after a while got up and walked around, putting myself in a state of hypnotic conviction that he would come here, come because he was Anthony, whose real name was Florus — yes, he had to come. When two hours passed and he did not come, I scolded him for being late. Just before midnight I heard him on the stairs, and when he came in and sat down, it was as if we hadn't parted, had remained together, talking for hours, and without any sparring around he told me he had made a plan. Tomorrow I was to find the man who had accosted me, get from him four hundred pieces of silver, and bring it to him. Then, very late tomorrow night, just before dawn, a wagon would leave the prison, and in the wagon, well covered, would be Simon, the Idumaean. At dawn the West Gate would be open, the wagon would pass through, driven then by the man who accosted me, or someone else chosen to take over, who would then deliver the four hundred pieces to the driver. Was this agreed?

It was agreed. He left and at last I got some sleep. Just before noon I was in the outer court of the temple looking for Isaiah and John and again had trouble finding them. Again a crowd had gathered. Word had spread that Herod's son, being just as astute as Pilate, had refused to get involved with the Galilean and the Sanhedrin. After having had fun with the Galilean, treating him as a clown, dressing him up and mocking all his pretensions, Herod's son had sent him back to Pilate, saying he found no threat against him in the man, and Pilate then sent him back to the Sanhedrin, asking them to reconsider their condemnation. Some in the crowd cried out that Caiaphas should accept the challenge and send the Galilean right back to Pilate and demand a death sentence.

I was glad to hear these things, for with anger spreading in the streets, the Romans would become watchful, all their attention on the streets, waiting at all hours for crowds to gather. No one would be concerned about a lone wagon going through the streets at dawn, heading for the countryside.

Simon's men found me, and when I told them the good news their eyes shone. Simon was like a brother to them, as he had seemed like my own brother when he had been seized, and I remembered this and wondered about it, for these men were not at all like my brothers; I respected them only for their courage and loyalty. I told them about the captain's plan. Isaiah said he would be ready to meet the wagon at the gate, then drive, and before doing so would hand over the four hundred pieces of silver. For my part, I said, I would hand over to the captain the four hundred I had in my house. We agreed John should be waiting with horses at the inn where we had often met.

Late that afternoon I met the captain in the tavern and handed him the bag of money, my own four hundred pieces, all my savings. "It is done," I said, and he said, "As the rest of it will be done." I felt no fear of this man, for how could he betray me without incriminating himself? Then, just in time, I saw some wondering suspicion come in his eyes, as if he were asking himself what my real interest was. And I said quickly, "I expect a share in this, you know." And grinning with relief he said, "You'll be looked after."

I went home, so exhausted I no longer cared what was going on in the streets, and ate well and drank, then fell sound asleep. It was broad daylight when I woke up. I lay for a while dreaming that by this time Simon would have reached the inn; by this time he might even be with his wife in the hills. I felt almost luxuriously lazy. Not till noon did I head for the Antonia. When I entered the courtyard and an officer asked if I had heard of the escape of Simon, the Idumaean, I could have danced on the cobblestones.

Then two hours later, the captain, looking for me, found me in my own place. Without a word he put his hand on my shoulder and left it there, his heavy hand, while he kept shaking his head as if struck dumb. Finally he blurted out, "I don't know what happened, Philo," and he told me a troop of mounted Romans, coming upon Simon some miles beyond the inn, recognized him, fell upon him, and brought him back to prison.

Wanting to kill him, I held his eyes because mine were so full of hatred, yet I couldn't frighten him — I think he wanted to laugh, I think he felt good. Never having been successful at anything in his whole life, he now had this triumph, a windfall of eight hundred pieces of silver without any real risk to himself; his escaped prisoner was safely back in jail. Nor could I cry out against him without incriminating myself. "And here's what's coming to you," he said, grinning. "A hundred pieces," and he handed me a purse. I had to take it, although I hated the feel of it in my hand. I couldn't even give the money to Simon's wife. I was involved in Simon's betrayal, she would say, and this money proved it. This blood money I held in my hand. Yet while feeling such hatred for the captain, I had to keep on smiling till he left, and then I threw myself on the bed.

Soon the terrible apathy overwhelming me left me utterly inert, too dull in the head even to despair. Then suddenly I couldn't stay there. Jumping up, I rushed out. It was early in the afternoon. Hurrying to Ezekiel's house, I found him relaxing in his beautiful garden with a jug of wine and a pretty young girl who was singing softly to him. With the blooming heavy flowers all around him Ezekiel rested and dreamt till I burst in on him, his wife trailing behind me. Startled, he stood up. I had to get control of myself, so before I spoke I tried to chuckle with amusement. "I knew you'd like to hear this, Ezekiel," I said. "I bring you news; indeed, I do." And carried away by my sudden blind desperate faith, I said I knew he would be as fascinated as I was. Simon, the Idumaean, had walked out of the fortress prison. Escaped right under the eyes of the garrison! Later, he had been recaptured out in the country, but no one knew how he had got away. The Romans were dumbfounded, and I had seen Simon in the courtyard, I said, when they were bringing him in, and Simon was laughing. "What a man! What audacity!" I laughed. Ezekiel laughed too; then, looking proud, he hurried in to tell his wife about it. The servants heard him, too, and I told myself, "See how the word spreads."

If my plan worked, by evening the whole town would be talking about Simon. Relaxing a little I plucked a big white flower, and while I buried my face in the heavy petals I could almost hear the shouting at Pilate; they would be shouting at Pilate, "Let Simon be the one. Free Simon. Free Simon."

XI

When I came home I knew as soon as I climbed the stairs that someone was on my heels. I kept wheeling around, but no one was there. In the room I listened, waiting, holding my breath; then came the knock on the door.

"Come in," I said apprehensively; then the afternoon sunlight from the window was on the bearded face and wild eyes of Judas.

"You!" I said. "What do you want?"

"Philo — now wait a minute."

"No. Try some place else." He stood in the doorway.

"You're a scribe, Philo. I come to a scribe."

"No, you don't. You can't hide here."

"Hide here? Hide? I'm not here to hide, Philo," and his superior air, in spite of the shape he was in, confused me. "I'm here because I want to have something taken down. A scribe, neither Roman nor Jew. Let me come in."

"All right," I said. "Come in."

Sitting in the room in the afternoon light he met my

eyes without embarrassment or shame, though all the marks of a shamed man were on him. He was unkempt, his hair uncombed and matted, and a big blue bruise on his cheek showed where a stone had hit him. The strain of exhaustion in his bearded face told that he had found nowhere to lay his head. And yet he smiled with the air of the superior man I had first encountered in the marketplace. He was looking around the room where he had helped me when I was sick. Here he felt safe. Romans were all around, the fortress just up the street. Yes, I thought, he knew where to come.

"Now look here," I said gruffly. "You're not my friend now. I think you're ruthless with people. I don't want to get involved in any way with you and the Galilean."

"I'm here to tell something that I want taken down. You're a scribe, aren't you? I'll pay you well."

"I don't want your money."

"It's the story. The real story."

"No one wants to hear your story."

"No one now. Ah, but later on . . ."

"Who'll care later on?"

"For a time — no one. But later on — at the right time — everybody. The love in the story — if the story's written down it'll exist somewhere. And as long as I know it's there — then some time — at the right time —"

"Judas — are you out of your mind?"

"I trust you."

"Well, I don't trust you," I said sourly. "You sold me out, too."

"Sold you out?"

"You certainly did."

"Mary, eh?"

"You deal in women, don't you?"

"You think I saw he wanted Mary for himself?" and he came closer, his eyes full of wonder.

"She took his eye, and you saw it. Why lie about it?"

"Oh, Philo," he began, and when he couldn't go on, the pity for me in his eyes confused me. I said nothing. Then, half to himself in a wondering tone, he said, "The girl was near the Son of God. The girl wanted to speak to the Son of God, and I was supposed to say, 'No, Philo wouldn't like it.' It's incredible." And as he faced me in his mud-spattered cloak, the wonder in his pity for me gave him a kind of grandeur. He believed in what he said, he believed with a sense of certainty that amazed me. Yet he was a well-travelled, educated man, and clever and worldly, too. I couldn't say anything. It was all too embarrassing.

"Look," I said gently, "why don't you sit down? Why don't you have a little wine? Take it easy. Come on," and I got the wine jar and a small bowl.

Drinking slowly, off by himself, he half smiled as if some strange fire in his head could now burn brightly. "Thank you," he said gently. "I know you'll bear with me just a little while. Thank you."

"Well, at least you've cleared up one thing," I said sardonically, indicating the bruise on his cheek and the dirt on his garment. "I thought the followers of the Galilean had all run away. I see there must be one or two around."

"Oh, more than one or two," he said. His hands, he had beautiful hands, held his head as he took the time to collect his thoughts. "Yes, bear with me awhile, Philo. You see, I expected all this. Oh, much more than this. I know it'll get worse for me. Yet, you know what's so strange? No one is really putting a hand on me."

I listened because he was taking my mind off Simon. If I listened intently I could keep Simon out of my mind. If they weren't touching him, what were they doing to him? I asked. Concentrating, he told me that when he walked along the street at night someone would come at him from a doorway. They came at him, yet no one touched him. No one put a hand on him — as if he would bring contamination to anyone touching him. From hidden places they threw rotten fruit and other things and he had to run.

Yet though they never came out of their doorways, he heard the tinkling of the little bells; bells for him and the demons. They kept hidden, as if knowing the time had not yet come — oh, he understood it, he understood it better than they did. Not yet. Not yet. Many voices came from the windows, then one big voice from a doorway, "Devils are near us on the street." And they tinkled their little bells; wherever he went he heard the tinkling of the bells.

In his own neighborhood, the Mount of Olives, where there were many followers of Jesus, children threw stones, then ran, the sound of the running feet driving him out of the neighborhood as if he were a leper. Now he had no place of his own, not after last night; his door had been pushed open, a man he could not see shouted, "Judas Iscariot . . . no one has been able to say who will be in hell — but now we know the name of one. Run there, Judas. Run." In the upper city, among the rich, there might be a place, if he could find it — up there they didn't care. But in the lower city the Galilean had followers keeping in touch and waiting. Keeping out of sight and waiting. For what? Well, I'd see.

And I felt all the fierce wounded pride in him as he said quietly, "I can't flee this city, Philo. Nor can anyone drive me away, nor will I collapse on the street. Not till some- one somewhere has my story." As he raised the bowl of wine to his lips, his hand trembled, but not from fear or despair, only physical exhaustion. Then suddenly there was exultation in his eyes. It made me nervous. Was there always this kind of excitement in these betrayals — successful betrayals? I wondered. Hadn't I seen exul- tant satisfaction in the captain's face after he had sold me out? The wallowing in a successful betrayal! And sud- denly I wanted to get rid of him. "If you act like a dog you get treated like a dog," I said sourly. "I've things to do, Judas. I've my own problems. Look, if you want a scribe there's one sitting down at his little table near the West Gate. He'll write you anything from a will to a marriage proposal. He's your man."

"It must be done in Greek, Philo. These things in Greek get read."

"Don't be such a fool, Judas."

"Who's the fool?" he asked softly. "Sooner or later everyone will want to know what really happened here," and as he came leaning close I thought he was deranged.

"This is not such a big story," I said. "Betrayal is such a common thing. It's all around us, in everything. Come on, in a little while this whole thing'll be forgotten." But I couldn't go on because of the sad pity for me in his eyes. Then his face changed, he was off by himself. Standing up slowly, he cried, "It's all right with me, I can stand it, as long as I know the truth is written and hidden some- where — for a time to come."

"Judas, Judas," I said soothingly.

"For a time to come, Philo."

"Look, you did what you did. Why not let it go at that?"

"I can't," he said. "Not after talking to Mary Magdalene."

"Mary Magdalene, eh? Very pretty, so they say. Is she one of your stable of women?"

"I have no stable."

"Did you bring her to him? Her too?"

"No, he found her himself."

"How? Tell me how."

"He came to her in a dream and — "

"Ah, I see, just like he did to Pilate's wife."

"I don't know. Did he?"

"He really gets around in dreams — his net of dreams. Is that how he took this woman away from you?"

"I used to drink with her, and him too, the three of us, laughing and drinking wine," he said, but then, growing deeply troubled, he hesitated. "You see," he said, "she was the only one who knew his mind as well as I did. I was sure he would have told her about me and the secret things. Now — I don't know. Maybe she wasn't to know. Not even her? Imagine. Well, I had to see her." A flush on his pale face now, he seemed to loom up over me, though I was sure he was no bigger than I. "Good God, that Mary could say it to me," he whispered bitterly, and closing his eyes he turned away, suffering from some intolerable humiliation. There were tears on his cheeks.

"Get hold of yourself," I said roughly, resenting him in this abject state. Staring at the door, he half rose, his eyes still on the door, as if he knew he should leave now, as if he were cursing himself for talking and for not being able to walk out. He said desperately, "I owe it to myself. Will you take it down?"

"I'm too busy now. I have other things on my mind."

"Philo, it's about what happened between me and the Galilean."

"I've heard what happened."

"No one knows what happened, Philo. Listen. He was like my brother — he still is."

"Come on. What is this?" I said.

"Ask anyone who really knows us," he said and as our eyes met I remembered him marching in that little parade with his serene and princely air, and I was troubled. "Whom will I ask?" I said.

"Ask Mary."

"My Mary, eh? Well, where is she?"

"Where you left her — I think."

"You think?"

"Well, it's your place and she knew you wanted her out . . . today. I was to take her to the Mount of Olives. I can't now. They won't let me."

"Then where is she?" I said. I couldn't believe she felt I wanted her out of that house at once, and yet I was hurt and suddenly very worried. I could see her waiting and waiting, then finally leaving, coming down the road, coming through the city gate alone, looking for a place for the night and the men at the gate watching her. And suddenly, all on edge, I couldn't sit still.

"All right, Judas. It's all right," I said. "All right," and I sounded so sensible he smiled. "But you're in no shape to work now — not until you rest, which is fine, because I have an appointment. You're safe here. So lie down and rest. There's a bowl there and a pitcher of water. Get some sleep while I'm gone."

"Thank you, Philo," he said. "It's very good of you," but the effort at a dignified air only made him look lonely and even more alone when he lay down, saying nothing as I left.

On the way up the hill to the Antonia stables I looked back, half expecting to see him following me, as Simon's wife did, out of loneliness. So I kept looking down the cold stone street. But stone is cold and lonely too. Bare stone houses, row on row, and it was as if a desolate, protesting cry followed me from my room.

I got a horse and rode through the streets on my way to the West Gate with the strong late sunlight putting a golden glitter on the hills and splintered rocks and on the stone houses too. The streets were unusually quiet in the beautiful afternoon peacefulness. Even at the temple courtyard only a few people stood around lazily in the warm amber light. Near the West Gate, the scribe, the one I had recommended to Judas, was at his table. Approaching the gate, I checked my horse to look at a woman bound and weeping, a poor creature suspected of adultery, her garment torn and held in place by a rope under her breasts.

The sun was going down when I drew near Mary of Samaria's house — my house — dismounting some thirty feet from the house near a tree where I could tether my horse. Then I saw two men and a woman coming out of the house and knew they saw me, too, for they stopped apprehensively. The middle-aged woman drew her shawl over her head, and the two men, sturdy and in their forties, quickly averted their faces, left the path leading to the house, and cut across the weeds to the highway. Followers of the Galilean, no doubt, I thought. What were they up to? Why even now did they run for cover?

I knocked on Mary's door, and there she was! Her

coppery hair was held back on her neck, and in her white robe she looked very clean and young, yet not quite herself.

"Mary," I said.

"What?"

"I'm glad you're here. That's all."

"I know I shouldn't be here, Philo."

"No. I want you to stay here. Mary, it's what I wanted to tell you."

"Everything here belongs to you, Philo."

"Stay here, Mary — make it your own place. Now wait," I said gently. "I won't bother you. I won't even come here unless you ask me to come."

"I see," she said. And then, troubled, "Why are you doing this, Philo?"

"I've loved you, Mary. Let me always remember you're here. All right?" As I stepped in I noticed a strange, hushed expectancy in her. I thought at first it had come from waiting to see what I wanted, and what I would do. Then I saw that this tension of waiting — this stillness that made her new to me and even more beautiful — had nothing to do with me. And I wondered if those people I had seen leaving had given her some mysterious upsetting message.

The strange expression on her face and the sense of expectation I felt in her confused me. What was the news? Did it give her hope? Was it news that her man would soon be free? Is that why she was keyed up and looking so glowingly alive, and full of that lovely freshness that had always rejuvenated me lying with her? Then, I lost my head. "Oh, Mary," I whispered, my hand going over her waist, her breast, her belly, as I trembled.

But I drew back and stammered, "I couldn't help it,

Mary. I've been so alone, I've been so worried. Everything has been going wrong for me.... Well, never mind. Now that I'm here you could give me a little information," and I sat down facing her.

"About what, Philo?"

"About a man you must know. A man named Judas."

"Judas!"

"Now wait, Mary. He wants to use me as a scribe for some kind of a confession. He's at my place now."

"Drive him away, Philo," she said, her eyes hard. "Drive him far away."

"It's a confession, Mary."

"Does he think that's going to help him now?" she asked, and in her eyes was something I didn't like, and again I wondered if the people who had just left had put a spell on her. "Leave him alone, Philo," she said in the same dull tone. "He might as well get used to being alone. He'll be alone in hell."

"I'd say it's all the more reason why his confession should be written down."

"What he says doesn't matter now, Philo."

"But he says he was close to the Galilean. No one closer. Is it true?"

"It's true all right. Some were even jealous of him. I would have done anything for him myself, and Jesus liked being with him. And they were so often together. I can't understand how Jesus could be so blind about him."

"Was it greed in Judas? Just greed? Or is it made to look like greed so everyone will understand it?"

"What?" she said, confused. "His people weren't poor."

"Who is he, Mary?" I persisted. "Has he a father and mother? Where does he come from?"

"They say he came from Cyprus." Then her voice

broke. I thought she was going to put out her hand to me, but she caught herself and said dully, "They're going to kill Jesus, aren't they?"

"No, no, Mary, I'm not even sure they want to kill him."

"Yes, they'll kill him, Philo. They have to kill him."

"Who will kill him? Only Pilate can condemn him. I'm not sure Pilate wants to kill him."

But she had started to cry, and I let her, and finally she said, "It's the waiting, waiting for him to die, that's so lonely." Then her hand, coming out impulsively, gripped my hand hard, and the feel of my hand, living flesh she had known, seemed to touch all the pride of life in her, and she wailed, "I don't want him to die." The wail brought me jumping to my feet. But just as suddenly she was quiet, and in the long silence, she was brooding, off by herself. Then her face suddenly brightened and I thought she looked a little mad. "It's all right," she said. "On the third day he'll rise and be here again."

"Mary, dear Mary — what are you saying?"

"It's all right now, Philo."

"Rise from the dead? Rise from the dead? Like Apollo's son. Oh, Mary."

"He said he'll do it. I know he can do it," and the exalted sense of expectancy in her face awed me. She *knew*. Judas! Now her! This land. The root of all Jewishness in these wild fantasies that could put us all under a blinding spell. Yet, I couldn't bear to hurt her. I said gently, "Do all his followers think he is to die, then rise from the dead?"

"They know it."

"Is it why they are hiding now?"

"Good-bye, Philo."

"No one really believes these foolish things, Mary," I

said gently. "It's not why they're all hiding. They're just scared."

"Good-bye, Philo."

"Stay here," I said gently. "As long as you want to stay, this place is yours," and bowing to her respectfully, I left her to her crazy dreams.

On my horse, trotting along to get into the city before dark, I tried to tell myself it was natural in her distress that she would have wild dreams that comforted her. But what were the followers of the Galilean up to now, I wondered. What was it they knew? Keeping out of sight, making no protest, waiting for a sign, and if it came, then what? Rioting? Insurrection? Everything suddenly seemed to be out of kilter and mysterious. The people of this land were full of wild fantasies. Yes, but how many fantasies had become more real to them than the simple facts of life? No one could have been more vitally alive, more sensually aware of all the natural things than Mary, yet look at her! Suddenly, to her, natural things weren't real. So who had any intelligence? And what good is a rational mind if it can't stand up against the fantasies?

And even Judas. At a glance, a highly intelligent man; I was good at this sort of quick assessment of a man's intelligence. How can you tell? The changing expressions, the change in the eyes, small revelations of superior awareness. And yet, this educated man, and Mary, an unlettered whore, were equally helpless against the Galilean magician's spell.

When I came through the gate in the last of twilight the sky had clouded up. It was a heavy, dark sky. Then darkness, with no stars and no moon, fell on the city.

The Antonia, high on the hill, was just a heavy darker blot, as was the temple. There was no skyline on the hills. Then lights began to twinkle all over the upper city. Soon the lights were arranged in patterns, tiers of light, rising from the valley, flickering flames from the oil lamps in windows. But at my place there was no light in the window.

Climbing the stairs, I listened, wondering how a man in such a frantic state could bear to sit still. Then I heard the sound of snoring, the long, loud, rattling snores of a man in deep sleep. I lit the oil lamp and there he was on the couch, curled up, just a heavy shadow, his face turned to the wall, and I had to shake him. "Judas, Judas, wake up." Turning on his back he stared up at me, the wide-open eyes full of his own strange world.

Saying nothing, he swung his legs off the couch and sat, his chin on his chest, looking so unkempt I got him the jar of water, the basin, and a comb, then watched him wipe his face and comb his hair. "Who did you see?" he asked.

"Mary of Samaria."

"Ah, Mary. Is she all right?"

"Well, she's still there."

"She's very lovely — very good," he said.

"Well, I'll remember her," I said cynically.

"No, you won't, Philo. No, she won't be remembered," and in the flickering light from the oil lamp there seemed to be a rapture in his smile. "I told you how these things live. It's the story — only the story that lives, Philo — if people like the story. Jesus knew this better than anyone, Philo. And it's why Mary of Samaria won't be remembered. Already someone else gets put into her story."

"What is this?"

"It's as I say."

"Are you out of your mind?"

"Ah, no, Philo; who's better than a Greek at myth-making?"

"Come on, what are you saying?"

"Haven't you heard? Well, the way they tell the story now, Mary Magdalene takes the harlot's place," and though he shrugged, I felt the excitement mounting in him, as if he believed he was getting to an important aspect of his own story. He insisted I was wrong in thinking that Mary Magdalene had been one of his women. Nor had she ever been a harlot. It was young Mary — my Mary of Samaria — who was the real harlot, the one who had wept at the feet of Jesus, washed his feet and dried them with her hair as he blessed her and told her she was beautiful now. A lovely sight it was, too. But already in the villages and in the countryside where Jesus had a great many followers, they were saying Mary Magdalene, whom they saw with Jesus all the time, was a repentant harlot who had fallen at his feet, weeping.

"I don't know why this story is more satisfying to them all," he said. "Isn't it fascinating? They want it to be this way. But why? Why do they like to tell it this way? Because the Magdalene was always with Jesus. Think about it, Philo. Go on. Well, it's the story they'll go on telling now, and so our poor Mary, the real whore with all that love, is now soon to be forgotten, Philo." After pressing his palms hard against his eyes, he fell into a silence and I waited. Then came that heartbreaking whisper, "Oh, I know these things have to be done now — for the sake of the ending — but to hear them say I was jealous and hated him, when I really loved and helped him."

"Helped him? Leading the Sanhedrin men to him?"

"You don't believe that story. I can tell you don't."

"Not that story. But Judas, listen. You took the money."

"The silver, yes," and he managed a weary smile. "You see, the story had to be believed. How do you make people, poor people, believe a man like me is a traitor? Show them he took money. The inducement all men, particularly the poor, believe in. So I asked for the silver. I took it. Well, it worked. Look at what they've done to me. Look."

What he said about the betrayal was only what I had said myself, but underneath his words were other words like a cry, a wild lonely cry; his desolate protesting eyes helped me bear it, and I motioned him to sit on the couch. Then, getting parchment from my desk and ink and pens, I told him I would make notes as he talked. Afterwards, I'd put the notes together, but this would take two or three days, then he could see the work and pay me.

Words poured out of him in such bursts of blazing intensity, I got lost in my note-taking and had to say again and again, "Now wait, Judas. Give me a chance." When he did heed me, I'd look up and see him lost in some reflections that moved him deeply. "All right, go on," I said. The notes were broken up, for often he would grow incoherent, and dwell at some length on incidents that fascinated him.

Later on, finding myself meditating again and again on his fate, I tried to straighten out the notes, and every time I touched them I could see him sitting on the edge of the couch, and if the truth wasn't shining in his face, I've never seen truth in a face. Here and now I try to let him tell his story, though it is, of course, strained through my memory. As I say, I still have the notes, but this is how I remember him telling it.

I first met Jesus when he was visiting his parents near Nazareth, and I was on my way to see the father of a boy I was tutoring. He and some of his friends had gathered at the crossroads and I, stopping to listen, liked his compelling style and presence.

He had a mixture of sweetness and solid strength that gave him a peculiar effortless dignity. He wasn't lecturing or arguing, just telling a story, but he was such a good storyteller he had me bemused by the story's implications. Drawn to him, I asked the man standing beside me who the storyteller was, and he said his name was Jesus, and he was his brother, and Jesus was the Messiah, and they were the sons of a carpenter who lived near by. The Messiah, mind you. Yet I didn't laugh.

When the storyteller had finished, I talked to him, but with some difficulty. I had a bad head cold, one of those summer colds that hang on. But in a few minutes he had made me feel he knew me from my birth. When I told him I had to go into town he said he'd walk with me, and I could tell him about myself. As we walked along in the dust and the sunlight, I told him how my parents had wanted me to be a great rabbinical scholar, so I had studied the law and the prophetic books, and being of a philosophical bent, I had read the Greeks and Romans, and how somewhere along the way my mind took another turn.

We walked, I talked. I became aware I was doing all the talking, yet doing it with a sense of ease and freedom. I told him I had figured out that my lonely wandering had begun on a feast day in Jerusalem when I had carried a lamb to the temple for the sacrificial slaughter. I remember that lamb. I remember holding it, stroking its head; with my other hand I could feel the fluttering of its heart, and that heartbeat became like my own heartbeat — brother hearts. Then my own wonder — life taking the form of a lamb, a bird, me, all united by our brother form. The dazzling variety of brother forms — all our throats being slit, the warm blood running on the altar. Was it really what God wanted?

In town, turning off the main road, we came to the little house where the boy lived. Jesus said he would wait, he didn't mind, he had much to think about. I talked to my student's parents, gave them my estimate of their son's character and the progress he had made, then came out and looked around for Jesus. Just along the road I saw a wagon drawn by a donkey in a ditch, a big wheel off, and Jesus was at the back of the wagon, trying to lift it high enough so that a boy, holding the big wheel in position, could shove it back on the axle. As I hurried toward them, Jesus was heaving and heaving, sweat rolling down his face, and just as I got there he cried, "Now," his whole body straining, his face red, and the boy shoved the wheel back on the axle. Sitting down, puffing hard, Jesus told the boy to run home and get a hammer, or the wheel would come off again. Then he smiled at us.

Waiting for the boy to return, we sat down on a big flat rock by the roadside, and as if we were continuing from the very point where we had left off, he asked what lands I had been in in my wandering. I told him I had been in Egypt and in Persia. I had loved a woman in Egypt, and still dreamt of a girl I loved in Persia. The same stories I told you here in this room when you had the fever. Remember, Philo, I wasn't sure you could follow me. Sometimes you seemed to be asleep.

I liked remembering. I say this now because he wanted to know what I had got out of my travels. He let me think about it a long time. Finally I said that looking back I remembered certain things with affection — things that at the time of the happening might have made me feel miserable, things that hurt — the pain sometimes in loving and parting and meeting again. In the end I knew I would have a fine life, if in the end I could have a good memory of things. That was the way it should be at the end of my life.

While I talked he made no comment, but in his silence, he had made himself my companion; he too was there. I had never known this kind of silence, so full of mystery.

But the boy had returned with the hammer, and Jesus, taking it, pounded at the wheel hub, fixing it so it wouldn't come off. Then, hammer in hand, he turned to me, the strong sun shining on his sweating face, and just as he turned, the donkey emptied its bowels. We all laughed. And with the steam from the defecation rising in the sunlight and the boy waving happily from the wagon, pulling away, Jesus said to me, "You heard my brother say I was the Messiah. Do you think so?"

"It may well be. I've never met anyone like you," I said, too quickly, so quickly it was embarrassing. I sounded like a lover. But he only smiled, putting out his hand, and invited me to walk home and meet his people. Yet he did not offer to cure my cold.

His father and mother, simple warm-hearted people in poor circumstances, embraced him warmly and welcomed me. They were like parents who had a brilliant son they adored without quite understanding him; this often happens in Judea where poor families have a son who is precocious in his studies. My own parents would have thought this father and mother uncultivated folk, but how would my own father have explained Jesus' commanding presence?

They gave me something to eat, and his mother made me a bowl of soup for my cold. When I was leaving, Jesus, taking my hand, said quietly, "You will be one of my disciples."

That night I couldn't sleep. My curiosity about him nagged away at me till my head ached, and waking suddenly, I wished I could see him near me.

Following him around the countryside, I met his other disciples. I was not one of them by temperament or training. They were all rude fishermen or workmen, sharing a splendor of purpose and devotion. Peter could direct men. John had a quiet sweetness. But their relationship with Jesus was different from mine. They listened in groups and learned and wondered, but I could take Jesus aside and talk to him about the world. He encouraged me in this kind of intimacy. I loved the times when he was alone with me. He said, "The isolated man can be blessed, Judas," and often he left me to lovely hours of solitary serenity. No one was closer to him — unless it was Mary Magdalene, who had become his companion.

This beautiful woman had a charming authority that made others step aside, for they knew she shared secrets with Jesus that he never revealed to them. I used to see them going off some place where they could have a drink of wine and be alone together. For my part I was never jealous of Mary. She was a woman, and he needed her in this company. But the others, who vied with each other for his attention, were upset by the secret place given to her, and they said to him bluntly, "Why do you love her more than you love us?" and he said, "Why aren't you more like her?" And Peter, in the Jewish custom, said, "But she is female, a female among men." Smiling, he jested, "When she is with us I'll make her a male."

Moving around the country, with the crowds getting bigger all the time, and making Jesus my whole life, I gained a secret understanding of him that dazzled my intellect. It seemed to me that he was bent on overthrowing the real masters of the world — the masters of the souls of men. In all those little stories he loved to tell dealing with people in their personal relationships, someone had to make a personal decision. A choice. In making the choice they learned something about themselves.

Yet there seemed to be no one right fixed road for them, no law of action. Not according to his own new law. And it was wonderful that this law wasn't to be just for the Jews. Who is my neighbor? he asked in the story about the Samaritan. Who then was a stranger? No one was a stranger, eh? And when he argued with the Pharisees at the temple, tripping them up, they were right in fearing him. Oh, they could divine that he was their mortal enemy. For them, you see, the truth was all in what had been done of old and written, and here he was saying his truth would set men free from all the prescribed forms. Yes, they suspected he was separating them from their subjects, the people — and they were so right. Again and again I expected to see him seized and brought to trial. He was reaching beyond the tribes and tribal laws to all mankind, the Jews at last simply part of mankind. Jesus in himself a new Passover — in a new flight to freedom.

I used to go off by myself, pondering over these things, saying over and over — the son of man — the son of God? Man and God. God in man, and I'd remembered he said heaven was not in the skies — if it was there the birds would know it — or in the waters, for then the fish would be close to it. It was within man. How marvellous — God was within me. Again and again, listening, feeling, concentrating, I said, "Yes, God is within me, and in everyone alive." Deeper and deeper I went into the dark caves within me. He was there, there for all of us, and I saw what Jesus meant, telling us to go off alone to pray in the silence of a room.

And the stories! How enchanted I was by his little

stories. Ah, Jesus and his storytelling! Those little stories, always so enigmatic. And yet I saw he was always saying the same thing in a hundred ways. Judge not lest ye be judged — be aware of the situation. I'm sure he was afraid he would be misunderstood and seized by the priests if he said openly, "I'm freeing you from the heavy bondage of the law — the one right action for every occasion." But when he dealt with that woman taken in adultery. You see, she should have been stoned, eh? Wasn't that the law? But what did he do? He said, "Let him who is without sin cast the first stone," and freed us from all the codes and judgments. The story stirred me and I asked myself, "What is involved here?" Awareness, yes, first awareness — without it there's nothing. Yet something else was involved. Compassion. Compassion and understanding overriding all legal penalties. The law no longer a tyrant. Freedom from the old tyrant.

I like wine. I've often been deep in wine, in the state of intoxication that makes the world a warm and lovely place, but I had never been so warmly lifted as I was now. I had not been drinking, yet I laughed as if I had been, thinking of those learned judges searching in their sacred books for the written correct penalties. At last they had become only a lower court, their judgments subject to the higher court — compassion — the court within oneself. My mind sang, my heart pounded, I was in love with the warmth and richness of life, but I also felt a humility strange to me.

My companions did not seem to have the imagination to share my insights. I loved them for their staunchness and their amazing willingness to accept in the most literal sense everything Jesus said, and I thought they loved me. But — well, education separates men, and some of my insights distressed them, particularly my view of what he meant saying he could overthrow the temple and rebuild it. This to me had a grandeur that was breathtaking; it meant that the temple could be destroyed and it wouldn't matter, he had moved it forever — into the heart of man. But the others, they couldn't see it. They were all so literal-minded, and I used to think it was because none of them knew the great sea.

I wasn't sure if Jesus had ever taken ship across the great waters. How could I know? There were years in his life he hadn't accounted for. But I felt the boundless, timeless vast seas in him, and one day, after we tramped along the road, and were resting, I intended to ask him about the great sea. I looked for him and found him sitting by a swiftly running brook with Mary Magdalene. Having taken off their shoes, they were sitting with their bare feet hanging in the water. The sun was shining on the white pebbles in the brook as they splashed their feet and Mary Magdalene was laughing, and Jesus, laughing too, touched the lobe of her left ear with his wet finger, and I withdrew.

One night at Bethany I wandered off by myself along the road from town and thought again of Jesus' handling of that woman taken in adultery. Thoughts about the woman led to thoughts about crime and punishment. It struck me that in all those little stories Jesus was telling us, right action depended entirely on the situation; there might be a different right and wrong for each situation. The action a man took had to come right out of the situation. And in life there were thousands of situations, none of them ever the same, since people were never the same, and so a man's life was like a river, a constantly changing river of adventures in freedom of choice and compassion.

Lost in my dreams, I stopped on the road, wondering where I was. It was pitch black. I looked up at the sky over the Judean hills, a sky filled with stars. Then I saw Jesus in each bright star as the canopy came down around me, and heard him in the deep night's silence like a majestic music, and felt him in a soothing, orderly rhythmic motion all around me, and he was in the earth under my feet, and in the cry of the night bird and each beam of moonlight on the low hills. And I, just a little speck on the road, was part of the great harmony of these things.

Coming to myself, trembling and awed by my awareness of a world in me as star-studded as any world in the heavens, I wept and would have done anything he asked me.

Along the way he did things I may not have understood correctly. The miracles! Why was he working the miracles? Oh, I could understand him turning water into wine; he loved life. From the beginning he was showing he loved life, and wine is one of the good things of life; I have drunk wine with him many times. And the healings — as if he thought he had to perform this magic for people who couldn't understand him. And raising Lazarus from the dead. Oh, this troubled me. Was Lazarus really dead?

I began to see a change in him, and was sure he was feeling sad about his work, and Mary Magdalene thought so, too, though great crowds followed him now — the poor, the lower classes. Did they expect him to lead them against their masters? All the priests were calling him a false messiah, and of course he seemed false to them. They thought they knew all about messiahs. In bygone days Cyrus, the Persian, had been hailed as a messiah because he could liberate all Israel and make Jews rich and powerful, but Jesus hadn't offered to make anyone rich and powerful. Watching him, I could see he knew he had to do something.

About this time he began to say he would die, and on the third day rise from the dead, as it had been written. The story was in the scriptures, he said, the story about the Messiah known by all men who knew the scriptures. As I have said, he did his teaching with stories because people like retelling good stories. The story lives on. So he was saying again and again, "I will die and on the third day rise from the dead." At first this troubled me, though I didn't know why. Then, believing I had discovered why, I grew frightened. Did he know people wouldn't go on believing in him unless he fitted into the great myth of death and resurrection?

One night I came upon him in the garden on the Mount of Olives, alone in the garden, in troubled prayer, and when he didn't heed me, I was so shaken I couldn't speak. After waiting a long time in the shadow, I heard him sigh, and the heavy sigh tore a wound in me. Then he said, "Yes, it must be done."

"What must be done?" I asked.

Motioning me to sit beside him, he remained with his head bent. Though neither of us said a word, I had never felt such a sureness of unity with him; it was like the night I had looked at the heavens, when I had felt myself carried away in a sweet harmony. I could hardly see his face. His hand came to my shoulder and I heard him say, "Someone must betray me. The story requires it. Now is the time. Which one of you, Judas? Which one?"

"No one," I whispered, but I could have cried out in my despair. In my love for him I began to weep and could say no more. In the dark he could not see my face, and he waited, and knowing he waited made me tremble, for I had known all along I would do anything he asked of me. I couldn't bear the ache in me. Then my love suddenly lifted into a wild abandonment and though still nothing was said, flashes of perception seemed to enlarge my understanding of the word "betrayal." The story as it had been written, yes, his followers needed it. The law, its codes. But he himself had said, "Judge not." For him there was only one law — love. Then maybe only one source of all evil — betrayal. The whole inner world swinging between love and betrayal — always first in a man's own heart. If it was time now for him to be betrayed, he would cause "betrayal" to be remembered with horror forever as the death of love.

My silence told him I would take on a burden none of the others could ever bring himself to take.

Shuddering, I told myself that it wouldn't matter what story they told, making me out to be the most loathsome of treacherous men — if he needed me. What did I matter? If I could do what needed to be done, though he wouldn't ask openly, then for his sake I would do it.

I shivered with a strange mixture of terror and exaltation. Rising, I took his hand, and he in turn put a hand on my shoulder.

The next day we were all at the supper table, all but Mary Magdalene, who had been helping prepare the food, and then he took up the bread and wine. In bread and wine was life, he said. His life and all our lives. Yet he would die. On the third day he would rise from the dead. He had often said this, he reminded us. But first one of us would betray him. Then, dipping the bread in the wine, he said he would hand the sop to the one who would betray him.

Aghast, they looked at each other. No one believed him. Then as he looked at me and our eyes met, my whole soul went out to him in secret acceptance of what was in that look, and he handed me the sop.

After taking the sop I waited, tense and trembling, for the others to cry out and rush at me, cursing, and drag me away some place where I could do no harm. No one lifted a hand against me. It was amazing. No one cried, "This shall not be." Yet Peter was a strong man, full of energy and decision. But now he seemed to be in a trance. They had all fallen into a trance. Neither John, who was so close to Jesus, nor his own brother offered to lay a hand on me. They had lost all sense of themselves, becoming, well, what? If they really believed that the treachery in my heart was now exposed, why didn't they cry out? Or were they under a spell?

"It is time, Judas," Jesus said, gently, and I left, trembling and wondering.

Going into the city I made my way to the house of Caiaphas, the high priest, where I asked the damsel at the door if I could see him on business of the gravest importance to all Israel. On being taken to him, I told him I was a disciple of the Galilean. But of course he knew this. And I told him Jesus called himself the Messiah and the Son of God, and Caiaphas knew this too. This powerful man of so few words simply appraised me as I talked, knowing all these things; then he said finally. "Yes, he's a blasphemer and should die."

At these words my heavy heartbeat cut off my breath, and right there I almost failed Jesus. My tongue was thick, I couldn't get it around the words, yet I summoned enough strength to say I would lead the Sanhedrĭn men to him, for a reward, and would identify him. When Caiaphas only brooded, saying nothing, I knew Jesus was well known to him after all the public debates and speeches, and that, like most of Jerusalem, he knew as well as I did where Jesus was. His manner fitted into the night's pattern, and this pattern began to frighten me. What we were all doing made me feel that I had become larger than myself.

Finally Caiaphas said, "It's better this way," and ordered that I be given thirty pieces of silver.

Then Sanhedrin guards carrying swords and

lanterns went with me to the house and garden where I had left Jesus and the others, and with their swinging lanterns casting strange shadows, the armed men burst in. Everyone in the room was frightened; they really seemed surprised, although they had been told this would happen. In a state of panic they held on to each other.

Then the captain of the guard asked in a loud voice, "Which one is the man we want?" And I went to Jesus and kissed him on the cheek. All my love was in that kiss, and I think he felt it, for at that moment he almost revealed the secret to the others. He said to the captain, "Why do you come like this, having me pointed out, as if you don't know who I am? You all know me. Haven't you all seen me at the temple preaching and talking? Why go through this?"

Then Peter seemed to wake up and, drawing his sword, slashed at the captain. When Jesus told him to put up his sword, Peter fell back into the frame of mind of the others which I can only call a trance. I felt we were all making rhythmic motions, a pattern, a kind of dance, a ritual dance, and now it was completed, and all the others could run away, deserting him — even as they are doing now and will go on doing till they see the sign.

Then the guards took Jesus away to the high priest's house. I was left alone in that room, the money in my purse. This thing was done that had to be done, and now I knew I must suffer shame and humiliation. But I counted on his love reaching and consoling me. In my suffering I would find the joy of serving him as no one else could have done. All night long I felt him beside me, consoling me, praising me. In the morning I tried to seek out the others. I sought them, one by one. But those who hadn't fled were in hiding, or those like Peter, denying they knew him, shunned me in horror.

Then I looked for Mary Magdalene on the Mount of Olives, waiting at the little house where she had been staying, which is near the house and the garden where Jesus had been seized. When she didn't appear, although it was already dark, I feared she too had fled. At last I saw her coming along the road in the moonlight, recognizing her by her proud bearing and easy rhythmic walk. She came closer, and her face was veiled and I had never seen her with a veil. Before I could speak, she stood back from me and said, "Judas, Judas, what drives you back to this shameful place?"

"To ask you one question, Mary," I said. "Do you believe it was as it appeared to be — a betrayal?"

"It is as they say it is," she said.

"You know me, Mary. And you know Jesus better than any of us know him. Could I really betray him?"

"Judas, a man is capable of anything," she said.

"Now listen, Mary. Listen carefully. Jesus is the Son of God, isn't it so?"

"It's so," she said.

"And the Son of God chose me to become one of his disciples. A Son of God — so blind to a man's character? Such bad judgment in the Son of God? It's incredible."

And she said, "I don't know what went on between you and Jesus. But it must be that he knew you were the only one who was capable of betraying him."

"I the one? What are you saying?" I shouted. "Look at me, Mary."

She stepped forward and lifted her veil, and in the moonlight I could look into her lovely face, so full of contentment that she was as she was — yet with the secret of some other place in her smile. And she took my head in her hands and kissed me — as a woman can kiss a man, with the most tender compassion. Yet I knew her compassion was not for the shame and suffering I now endured, but for the man I was or am. I cried out, "No, Mary, no!" but, veiling her face again, she entered the house and I heard the bolt on the door.

Because I was the man I was! No! Because I am the man I am. That kiss! I pounded on the door. My whole sense of myself was so shaken I trembled. Every man is capable of anything, under the right pressure, I know all that. But to say that the others, all his other companions, could be seen as incapable of betraying him, and they would die first, while I... Why? Because I've travelled more? Because I've seen great cities, loved more women, had more money, been cut off from my family, read more books, and can talk more philosophy? More! More of everything. Is this my great flaw? In me more of the human chaos, rage, hate, anger, selfishness, pride, meanness, generosity, love. More love for him ... Ah, is that it? So I'm picked as the one who, even if he does not do it, is at least capable of doing it. It's an insult — it's a knife thrust at my throat....

Look what's going on. Peter runs around now denying Jesus, others hide. Could I deny him now? Never.
Never. Never. Yet if Mary is right — if Jesus picked
me in the beginning because he knew I at least was
capable — the flaw in my nature was seen. Everything that makes up a man in me was seen — and
from the beginning I was used. Used by the Son of
God, picked out to be the victim.

I don't believe it. I know my own heart. I know
I'm incapable of being treacherous to Jesus, and he
knew it — which is why he turned to me. Isn't that
the truth?

This is the story Judas told me in the half darkness of my
room with night coming on, and when he had finished
he stared at me for a long time, tears streaming down his
face. Suddenly he stood up, clenching his fists, raising
his arms high. His eyes frightened me. I thought he was
making some wild protest. Then just as suddenly he
changed, dropped his hands, and began talking to himself, nodding and nodding; then I could hear him whis-
ering, "No, only the story Jesus wanted told. And I'm
willing. I'm serving him willingly. What does it matter
what happens to me?"

Trying to control a tremor running through him after
a convulsive sob, he couldn't face me. And I was glad he
couldn't, he was so utterly shattered, and I was so shaken
myself. "Why does this have to be?" he whispered.
"Why? Oh, Lord, I know why. And yet why, even though
I know?" Some other things he said I couldn't hear, but I
did hear this: "And now he'll suffer. There'll be terrible
suffering, and I'll endure it with him. And worse, oh, my

God, I'll be blamed for it — as I'm blamed now. Jesus, yo
loved me as I love you. What kind of people need all th
to believe in you?"

Then he sat on the couch, holding his head in h
hands, and I said nothing. I couldn't. Never in my life ha
I stood near a man who in his silence and sudden stillne:
showed suffering like this that drew me into such va:
frightening loneliness. I was glad when he raised h
head. He looked at me, just looked at me steadily. The
he cried out, "Don't you understand?" and he jumpe
up. "Someone somewhere must know the true story -
even if it can't be told for a long time. Do you hear m
Philo? If truth is in love, then after this thing is done an
told about, the truth should be kept somewhere. Believ
me, Philo. Only you can keep it now. Do you hear?"

"I hear you, Judas," I said soothingly. "I'll write it dow
It'll be kept."

"Thank you," he said.

"Good," I said, and though I believed in his sufferin;
he had so upset me I couldn't make up my mind wheth(
the suffering came from shame or love. I wasn't eve
sure I believed his story.

"Well, where do you go now?" I asked.

"I have nowhere to go. Wait — in the lower city there
an old Canaanite woman who nursed me when I was
child. She neither knows nor cares anything about the:
things. I left the money with her. I can sleep at her place

"I'll walk out with you," I said. "I haven't eaten sin(
this morning."

I told him he could feel secure, no one would recogni:
him in this neighborhood; he could go on his way. I di
not ask him to have a very late dinner with me, thoug
he must have been hungry. But how could I ask him

How could I let myself be seen with him — a marked man now? Already I was heartbreakingly involved with one doomed man, Simon.

I had followed Judas out, and as he turned to go down the street, I called, "Judas —"

"What?" he said.

"Do you still think he can do it?"

"Of course he can."

"Tell me then, how will he do it?"

"I told you," he said, his eyes full of disdain. "He's the Son of God."

And he left me, and I knew that I should not be standing there watching him go down the street, hearing in my heart that wild, protesting, desert cry. But then, still watching, I grew fascinated. He didn't look back. There was nothing furtive about him as he went on down the street. His head was held high. His stride was firm. A proud man again, he didn't care now what happened to him.

Then I knew that if there had been one person in the world who knew his heroic story he would have suffered any shame, any torment — endured it all and been satisfied with it all, and would never have come looking for me. In his heart he must have secretly counted on that one person being his pretty woman friend, Mary Magdalene. And now, though he would not turn as I went on up the street, I felt him following with his eyes.

XII

He more than followed me with his eyes; he might just as well have followed me into the tavern, for while I was eating he loomed up in my mind. And the more I thought of him, the more I wished I had given him shelter and shown more sympathy. The passion in the man, the purity of feeling that had made the world new for him, touched half-forgotten things in my youth — like those days when the sun setting on a dark sea, or a flower held in my hand after a rain, in sudden sunlight, seemed so beautiful and painfully close to me. Beauty that hurts, so new it hurts.

After eating I sat sipping my wine, wondering what some of my scholarly friends in Rome would make of Judas. Some would call him a lonely discontented Jew trying to find the wings of freedom in his hero, the Galilean. Yet in Alexandria, where I had some Greek friends who were far more skilled in speculation than those Romans, and more cynical too, they would take delight in Judas's question, "Because I had more love, was I therefore more capable of betraying him?" Ah, interesting! Interesting! Betrayal as an aspect of love. One of the aspects of love, food for a long meditation. But how could the Romans, who had so amazingly opened their arms to the fantasies of the whole world, ever understand this one Jew?

I had frightening problems of my own. As I was leaving, two well-dressed merchants, who had been sitting with their backs to me, also left. On the street, just outside the door, they turned. Isaiah and John. "Philo, dear Philo," Isaiah said. The good clothes had been stripped, no doubt, from some rich merchants months ago, and now, in step with me going down the street, they were like two men who just happened to be going my way. Further down the street were three other men, a little drunk. I had told Isaiah never to wait for me outside my house. "How did you know where I was?" I asked, and he said, "Oh, we keep track of you, Philo."

Then John asked when Simon was to die. I told him I didn't know.

Walking in the middle of the road past darkened doorways and dim lights in windows, I felt a little chill of apprehension, knowing I would have been frightened if I could have seen their eyes. Even in the silence, violence touched me. I asked quietly what they wanted. Did our friend the captain ever journey from the city? Isaiah asked. If he did, it was up to me to keep track of his movements. The first time he ventured into the countryside he would be killed. Who could object? I said. But they might have to wait! The captain rarely journeyed to other towns. What else was there to wait for? John said.

A little further on, Isaiah said casually that the remnant of Simon's band wanted him to be their leader. As I turned quickly to John, he nodded. "It's your business," I said. "Yours too, Philo," Isaiah said, and told me I could be just as helpful to him as I had been to Simon. As it was, they needed money badly. The captain had got the money Simon's wife had saved, so it would be my job to meet them as I used to meet Simon in the marketplace, or wherever was convenient, and I could continue giving accurate information about the movements of richer caravans on the highways.

His calm, flat self-assurance shattered me. I was to be his man now, he had hold of me. In my sudden uneasy awareness that he was in my life now, I put my hand on the hilt of my sword, wishing I could see his eyes. In the shadows he was just a big heavy form, the smaller John half-hidden behind him. A silence fell between us, and in it I seemed to know much more about him than I had before. He had never liked me. A powerful utterly ruthless man, he had an incredible primitive loyalty to one other man, Simon, and he knew Simon loved me. That was his problem. He had no interest in priestly disputes or refinements of the law. A farmer, a peasant turned thief, he knew only that he was a Jew with a tribe, and that I was the ancient stranger in his land. If it weren't for Simon, he would cheerfully cut my throat, and as a bit of the night light caught his eye, I half expected him to accuse me of having collaborated with the captain. "We'll get the money back, and we'll get more," he said quietly. "Say when we'll meet, Philo."

Since he made no threat, I could have believed for a moment our shared love for Simon and our hatred of the captain held us together. No, not this man. Of his own accord he would share nothing with me. For a few shekels he would reveal my relationship with Simon, if Simon were dead. While Simon was alive, he would not do so; it seemed incredible that this ruthless and brutal man could not betray me while Simon's affection was there.

As the three drunken citizens ahead of us on the street started to sing, then disappeared into a darkened doorway, I told Isaiah he would have to give me two or three days before looking for me in the marketplace. At my house they did not loiter, but went on their way, and I got to my room and flopped in a chair.

Suddenly I jumped up, drew my sword, slashed at the air savagely, and kept on slashing. I was good with the sword. Isaiah was a very foolish man if he thought his bulk and muscles could match my sword — unless he got me in the back. After running my thumb along the edge, I put up the sword with satisfaction, but as I picked up the Judas notes there was a pounding on my door. At last the pounding I had heard so often in my dreams! But even now it was strange to hear it sound so like the pounding I had expected for so long. I jumped up, assuming immediately that Isaiah and John, having been seen with me and recognized in spite of their rich clothes, had been seized, and had talked.

I opened the door, and the young Roman, Felix, from Pilate's own guard, said, "Be quick, Philo. Pilate wants to see you."

"So, Pilate wants to see me. Good. Let's go," I said. I wanted to behave well.

Going up the hill, my eyes on the dim lights in the massive fortress, I kept joking with Felix. I made him laugh. He looked like a fair-haired blue-eyed German, but had been born in a little town not far from Rome. Sounding like a courtier, I asked if Pilate was in a good mood. No, Felix said, the procurator's mood was vile. The Sanhedrin had had the audacity to send the Galilean back to him, demanding that he be put on trial for his life.

XIII

My common sense told me that if Pilate had concluded I had a business connection with Simon, my situation was hopeless. For, having condemned Simon to death, he would want to be even harsher with me. If he had made up his mind about me, I knew no one could save me, any more than my joking and laughing with Felix as we entered the fortress could save me from the panic growing in me. Struggling desperately against this panic, I puffed myself up, finding courage, even bold confidence, by telling myself that I had powerful friends in Rome — I was not a nobody to be tossed to an executioner. I could tell things some powerful Romans would not want to hear told, and they would know this. The senator had found great allies coming to his aid when we needed them, and he would bring them to my aid now. It was incredible they would let a man like me be killed out here in Judea over a small share in a corruption that was general, and so Pilate would have to listen and give in to them.

But as soon as we reached the apartments the puffed-up sense of my importance collapsed. I told myself I was out of my mind. No one could budge Pilate. I had seen this during the riots. Forces far more threatening than anything the senator could muster in Rome had come against Pilate. I had read the letters from Rome. I had answered them for him. Harsh letters. Then the fury of the Sanhedrin. Then the rich Jews in Rome, so influential there, who tried to get him recalled. He had been satisfied in his conscience he was right. Oh, Pilate's terrible, frightening conscience. Pilate was my fate.

But as I shivered, giving in to my panic, I seemed to hear him laughing; wonderful, comforting laughter suddenly picking me up. And I remembered he really could listen; he could be made to change his mind, too, if it wasn't set. I had seen it happen during the amazing riot over soldiers carrying banners bearing the imperial image. All this fuss over an image, and he had laughed. I was there, I heard him laugh and say, "They call this nonsense about an image religion? If this is interfering in their religion, all right, get the banners off the streets. Make them happy. What kind of a god is this? Where did they get him?" And remembering this, and thinking, too, how like him it was to want to question me for himself — if his mind wasn't made up — I was buoyed up.

I was glad, too, that the apartment was furnished like a fine Roman home, free from clutter and oriental opulence. We could have been back in Rome, where we both had good friends. But he left me standing ten feet away from him, my heart pounding while he leaned back in his chair meditating. My eyes shifted around the room, looking for guards ready to arrest me. But only his wife was there, reclining on a couch near him and watching me soberly. "Philo, come closer," he called, his tone friendly. Then, glancing at his wife, as if they were still pursuing a conversation, he said he understood I had been in this land many times and knew about Jewish religious feelings — and I'll remember to my dying day my trembling relief and the wild whirl in my head when I saw I was not to be questioned about Simon. Instead, he was saying, "Sit down, Philo. Tell me what you make of this Jewish God. What you yourself have discovered."

I did sit down, but waiting for my head to clear, I could only stammer. It seemed incredible that I had been brought here at this hour to be questioned seriously by the procurator, and in the presence of his wife, on things Judas had talked about such a short time ago. It was as if the Galilean still troubled Pilate and his wife almost as much as he troubled Judas, although Pilate had questioned him at length a few days ago. I was as moved now by Pilate and his wife as I was by Judas, and I didn't know why.

While I remained tongue-tied, Pilate, thinking I was intimidated in his presence, kept nodding encouragingly. Even so, I couldn't get going. I talked perfunctorily about things he must have heard many times before; how Yahweh, some said, had been a minor thunder god in North Africa until the Jews had taken him over; and I went on about my reading of the Jewish prophets, and how I had delighted in the splendid poetry, which, of course, was tribal, always tribal, and then, beginning to warm up, I said I had made some fascinating discoveries; when these poets sang, "O Israel," they were really singing, "O Lord God," as if Israel and God were the same thing. It was the same in all their books. Searching for a Yahweh who was a divinity apart from the people, I always got the same impression. Yahweh wasn't a god as Jupiter was a god, nor was there any world of the gods which the Greeks and the Romans often see as a playful place. For Yahweh there was no other people — only the Jews. None before. None after. Taking my time, utterly at ease now, I asked: "What if Yahweh is simply an aspect of the Jewish mind? What if he is merely their sense of themselves?"

The talk with Judas was so fresh in my mind, with Pilate and his wife listening so intently I got carried away. I found myself saying, "I met a young Jew, a scholar, who told me he had asked himself once, 'Where is Yahweh?'" Then I caught myself. But Pilate, his large eyes first on me, then on his wife, smiled faintly. Was Judas still moving me? I don't know. But I could have cried out, "What is on your mind, Pilate? What troubles you about these people and their religion? And the Galilean? You are a Roman. Leave them alone. Don't get in the way."

But Pilate said, "The young Jew who asked where is Yahweh — yes, Philo . . . go on."

I talked about this young Jew as if I had known him all my life. A poet, yes, he must have been a poet, whose wanderings began when he asked where God was, and thought about the sea. He had talked to me about God, the tribes, and the sea, and how the minds of the tribes would have been shaped differently if they had come from the sea, not the desert.

My thoughts now seemed to come from Judas, and Pilate's wife raised her head in surprise. "The sea?" she said softly, "the sea." "Yes, the sea," I said. Ports on the sea, ships with strange cargoes from faraway lands and sailors speaking strange tongues. The Greek mind is so full of curiosity, I said. It is always reaching across seas. But the Jewish mind, I went on, always turns inward. It's land-locked. Its hungers and satisfactions are born of desperate desert thirst; a mind from the beginning locked too long in the desert, a spirit molded in isolation.

Oh, I know the desert has its own beauty as strange as the sea's, I said, but a beauty of sand and crags and bare cliffs and fantastic mirages and flaming flowers rooted in light on dust storms. The mind playing tricks. Illusions. The tricks come from shifting light blazing on rocky crags, creating illusions. Light on an eye turned inward, giving isolated lonely men grand mirages so beautiful they thirst, then they kneel down and put out their hands. But what do they have in their hand? Sand. Grit.

So the minds of these men have to have a Yahweh; they have to find him in their own minds, not in the sand. So they can nurse in the desert a sense of preferment, so they can have a feeling of being chosen even in their desert isolation. For just as the cruel desert is against them, aren't all the world's people to be against them? Why? Their sacred sense of preferment. All this drilled into them in the desert by ruthless chieftains, the priests who hold the power.

"Then Yahweh is not in the temple?" Pilate asked.

"Only when the Jew is in the temple, I think," I said smiling, and Pilate's lovely wife, who hadn't spoken, put a pillow behind her head, shifting her body, her face changing too as if I had said something that proved her right in an argument with Pilate; and her eyes told me to go on.

The fascinating aspect of the thing was, I said, that if Yahweh was merely the collective consciousness of the Jews, then their worship of him was really worship of themselves. Well then, how to control themselves? And who was to have the control for all time? Well, here the priests, it seemed to me, had performed a feat of magic Greeks and Egyptians should envy. The priests dug up Yahweh's law book somewhere. Think of it. Their god or their priest telling them there was a right way and a wrong way to act on every single occasion — as it was written. All of life, all human behavior, under a tribal rule. A man washes his face, a woman takes a bath, a child crosses the road in the one and only way God wants these things done. Never another way, I said.

And I had read that this magnificent codification of life had been found at a time when the kings in Jerusalem took delight in pagan things, and old gods were found in old sacred groves. Things were badly out of control . . . but now, having the codes . . . the law . . . everything to be done as it was written it should be done. What a fascinating discipline for holding the tribes together. What a drill. What a subjugation of all that's spontaneous in the heart. The perfect captivity, I said, shrugging. But, of course, in this captivity they quarrel fiercely among themselves.

I had lost Pilate, who frowned, off by himself, so I turned to his wife. But Pilate said, "I asked you, Philo, to tell me about the Jewish God. Instead you talk about the Jews."

"It's the same thing," I said.

Paying no attention to me, he stood up and walked slowly by the couch where his wife reclined — she was as baffled as I was — and making a circle around the couch, before continuing on his way, he went toward the door. Then, returning to his chair, he repeated the journey around the couch before going back to the door.

"I see what you mean, Philo," he said. "If I had to leave this room every day of my life, and each time I left, it was my habit to circle that couch on the way to the door, then the day might come when I couldn't feel free to leave the room unless I first circled that couch. By then the pattern is set in my mind and it's my prison. I'm a captive."

"It's true."

"And if I didn't do it I'd feel guilty."

"That's also true."

"It would become a religous thing. A rite. And not to do it — blasphemy! A blasphemy."

He sat down, brooding, and as he sipped his red wine, his face hardened. Finally his wife put out her hand, and looking up, he took her hand, sighing, and said courteously, "Thank you, Philo." But as I left, I wished I hadn't given an honest view; it might have pushed him in a direction he was inclined to take anyway, a dangerous direction which could destroy him and his wife. The only time she had spoken she had repeated "the sea," with eagerness in her eyes.

XIV

Leaving the fortress, I felt almost happily secure; Isaiah wouldn't betray me while he could use me, and he had to try and use me because he was so desperately in need of money. And as for Simon, I was awed by the man's loyalty to me and his own sense of himself, facing death. The shadow of his approaching death, the place and time not named yet, aroused in me the frantic need for the consoling quickening I could only get from a woman. Aspects of love, I said to myself, thinking of Judas earlier in the tavern. Aspects of longing. Longing for what? There was a young Canaanite girl in the lower city whom I had often visited before taking up with Mary of Samaria, and now, heading for the Canaanite part of town, I went down by the temple wall, then across the valley, then into the neighborhood where Canaanites had lived for hundreds of years — a poor desolate remnant of a city that they had once ruled. Since it was late at night the neighborhood looked better than it did in the day. It was a slum, and it smelled like a slum. The narrow stone lanes had a scum on the stone, dust and soot from the close cooking fires; in the day the only light came from the overhead ribbons of sky, winding canals of hard glaring light. More than that, more than the slums of Rome and Athens and Damascus, there was a shabby, mean, desolate air here, a sour smell in the spirit, vinegar and charred wood, dung fires. The Canaanites — laborers, small craftsmen, or little shopkeepers — were all poor and without any influence in the priest-ruled Jerusalem. I had heard that many Canaanites were followers of the Galilean, who had talked about his love of the poor, and according to my physician friend had said there would be no place for the rich in his kingdom.

Encountering no one on the dark streets, I came to a courtyard like all the others. On the street level were tiny little shops, and above these shops, living quarters that extended all around the courtyard. Families lived in rooms like rabbit cages that were even smaller than the tiny little shops. But in the daytime the families had the courtyard and the sunlight.

In the dark I climbed a stair and, going deeper along the row of rooms above the courtyard, I tapped on a door. The little Canaanite girl, being a prostitute, had a tiny room to herself, apart from her family, which she always kept very clean. The respect with which she was treated by her neighbors may have come from a racial memory of the ancient days of Canaanite glory in Jerusalem when the prostitute had been a sacred figure in their temple. Tapping and tapping, I finally woke the girl, a streak of light appeared under the door as she lit a candle, and then she came, rubbing her eyes and yawning. "Philo," she said in surprise, then her smile in the candlelight was beautiful.

After smoothing the covers on her bed, she got a bowl of wine and we drank, then caressed each other. Young as she was — she was seventeen — she had the skill of a priestess who knew how to turn the dark into a sudden blaze of light. But I couldn't go on in this dalliance, I was greedy for her. Then, when I lay quietly beside her, she turned the relief I felt into a great luxury, massaging with erotic skill my neck and shoulders. "Why are you so tense, Philo?" she asked. "What's been worrying you?" The wisdom in her eyes was in her fingers too. She rubbed sweet-smelling light oils on my neck, chest, and shoulders. She combed my hair. I emptied my purse for her, putting the coins by the thick candle, leaving her in her bed.

It was a chilly night. On my way out I went down through the courtyard, stopping by the fire that burned there. The heat from the leaping flames put a fiery glow on the half-shadowed faces of eight or ten men squatting around the fire, and made them all look fierce. No one paid any attention to me. I caught only snatches of their excited talk. "Well, first he has to die." "Oh, he'll die. Didn't he say they'd kill him?" "What if they don't kill him?" "If they don't, he can't do it?" "Nobody rises from the dead. Nobody." "It's why he'll try to do it." "If he can do it, it's the sign, isn't it?"

And as the flames shooting into the shadows made their faces glow so fiercely, my mind whirled. I thought I could hear a voice in the distance. "He's risen, he's walking the streets again. See, he's really the king," and I saw thousands of these wretched Canaanites rushing from their hovels, joined by thousands of poor Jews from the lower city, all rushing to the temple courts, and joined there by thousands of peasants marching on the city.

Then, shuddering, I fled. The Galilean was still alive, he hadn't even had a trial, yet these people were counting on his being killed, so they could see what would happen after his death.

XV

Since I was a scribe and an interpreter, no one questioned my right to be at the Galilean's trial along with one or two Roman officers who were interested, and the small company of Roman soldiers who always attended Pilate on these occasions. In the fortress judgment hall there were no Jewish spectators. But outside in the courtyard were four or five hundred, murmuring as a crowd murmurs, an excited shriek sometimes breaking the wave of murmuring — or one sharp vindictive cry.

Pilate in his blue robe came into the hall, walking slowly to his place in the great chair on the dais. And as he looked around, an expression on his face I could not fathom, he was almost splendidly aloof and magisterial. If I hadn't known him I would have said his aloofness was born of a superior resentment at being forced again to face this predicament. When the Galilean had come before him a few days ago, he had examined him, and found him rather peculiar, but blameless. Then he had him sent back to the Sanhedrin, telling the high priest to

deal with him according to their own law. It wasn't his
business. Now the Sanhedrin, sending him back to Pilate
for trial, was demanding he be condemned and executed;
something they did not have the power to do themselves.
We all knew this. We all knew that Pilate was being told
what he must do according to the disposition of power in
the city. He had signed the order for Simon's execution
without showing any interest in the matter. Death sen-
tences, executions carried out according to Roman law,
meant nothing to him. Simon had meant nothing to
him. This was different.

Now up there on his dais he did an odd thing. Linking
his hands, he looked at them as if from a great distance,
waiting, saying nothing. There was such tension in the
folded hands and the silence, I was full of foreboding.
Finally he gave a signal. The Galilean was brought in,
and I looked at him for the first time.

Bound like a dangerous criminal, a soldier on each
side, he wore his own clothes, a plain brown coat and a
countryman's shoes. My first thought was of his shattering attraction for Mary of Samaria that made me nothing
beside him. I couldn't see anything in his bearing to
make a woman turn and look a second time. Maybe this
was because he had red marks on his face from having
been slapped hard. Yes, good-looking, but not strikingly
handsome. He had interesting eyes, and black hair, not
cropped like Pilate's, but like Judas's, and he had a short
beard. Yet Judas thought this man was the Son of God.
According to Judas he had a soothing hypnotic presence.
But not for me. Not now; from where I stood, I couldn't
feel any magnetic pull at all.

In all fairness, maybe as yet no one here had caught
his eye. His eyes weren't on anyone. He might just as

well have been alone in the hall, standing manacled, steeped in the contentment of his loneliness, and in my mind's eye I saw behind him that fire in the Canaanite courtyard, flames flickering on faces, and I heard the voices, "Rise from the dead, you say. Well, we'll soon see if he can really do it."

This man in the brown coat? Was he a magician? Magicians can go quite mad. Was he mad now — like the magician I knew in Alexandria, a squat bald man with a huge torso bearing a hundred wounds from spikes half driven into him? He had mastered pain and control of the blood's circulation. Drunk with his power, he claimed no one could kill him, and, appearing before a great crowd, he had a soldier hurl a spear at his chest. I saw the mad pride and exultation in his face as the soldier threw the spear from twenty feet away. The spear dug into his chest, and he fell. The crowd, cheering wildly, waited for him to get up. But he was dead.

Now, Pilate, in spite of his close questioning of the Galilean a few days ago, looked at him with much curiosity as if he had never seen him before. And maybe he hadn't — not as he was seeing him now. The questioning had been more like a conversation, I had heard from Felix, and in the end, Pilate did not know what to make of him. He had felt no threat to Rome in him, or to the Sanhedrin, or to anyone else. Impious men, even in Greece, have always been considered a threat to the state. Yet now Pilate was studying the Galilean as if he saw him in another light. Maybe the Galilean's bearing, the sense of terrible isolation he conveyed, reminded Pilate of our talk last night, as it did me, and he saw how the Galilean now fitted so perfectly into that desert picture I had drawn. Looking at him again myself, I, too, saw all those ancient wilderness figures behind him. I saw him sharing with them here the desolate loneliness of bare cliffs, crags, and strange lights on dust storms, flaming mirages floating ahead on swirling dust. Mirages, beckoning, and bringing him here where his hand reached out — and now — just sand. Sadly, oh, so sadly, just the sand of this judgment hall. And Pilate took a long time, too, looking at him, then almost gently he asked who would make the charges.

When the two guards stepped aside, leaving the Galilean alone, three of the higher priests came in.

Caiaphas wasn't with them. I knew the plump one with bells on his coat and a grand authoritative manner, and the other too, a bearded hawk-nosed fierce-eyed old man. But I did not know the third, who was younger and richly dressed, without the little bells, and full of priestly success. He was the one who began to recite the charges. When he had finished, the others spoke in turn, each one saying, "He calls himself King of the Jews and is in rebellion against the state," and listing other charges as well; the Galilean was a blasphemer, who, they said, called himself the Son of God, called himself, too, the Messiah, and had proclaimed also that he could topple the temple and rebuild it in a day, charges that merited the death sentence after the condemnation by the Sanhedrin.

They were very clever in accenting the charge that he had called himself King of the Jews, and had even come into Jerusalem hailed by his followers as King. In this way they kept trying to involve the Romans in the charges, for if Jesus had proclaimed himself King, then indeed he was a threat against the state, and the Romans themselves should deal with the rebellious man, and if he were guilty of rebellion, Pilate would not be ordering an execution merely to carry out the Sanhedrin's will. They spoke well, showing great deference to Pilate, implying that their concern was only the security of the state. And Pilate listened carefully.

But the younger one whom I did not know, proud and handsome, whose eyes could blaze, whose voice could shake, took a different tone as he pointed at the Galilean. Yet he smiled a little, nodding, nursing his own deep understanding of what was involved here, facing Pilate like an equal, demanding that Jewish rights be respected. Blasphemy was a crime against the Jewish religion and therefore a crime against the Jewish state. Since the Sanhedrin had examined the Galilean, and condemned him, as was their right, since this was a matter entirely within their province, they were behaving correctly in asking Pilate to pass sentence on him, for it was not in their jurisdiction to do it themselves, according to this distribution of power. He said he could not imagine Pilate choosing to disregard the Roman respect for the Sanhedrin's right to condemn one of their own people for a religious crime. Why should he do so? What else was involved here? And Pilate, listening, slumped in his chair, rubbed the side of his face, which was entirely impassive.

While being harangued by the young priest, Pilate kept his eyes on the Galilean. Now I too looked at him. Standing there in his brown coat, his hands tied behind him, he had hardly noticed how the young priest had kept pointing at him, nor did he meet Pilate's eyes, or even glance around the hall at the soldiers. If he had slumped, if his body had sagged, I would have said he was bored, or indifferent. He stood straight, yet apparently lost in thought. Then suddenly he did look around almost in surprise, a stranger, asking himself what they were all doing here.

Then Pilate said to him urgently, "Answer them. You must answer them."

Turning to the priests, the prisoner said, "I have preached in the temple. You all know me. You've listened to me. Which one of you heard me say the things you say I said?"

The three priests, putting their heads together, whispered furiously for some time and the young man, making an angry slashing movement with his right hand, took the plump older one by the arm as if he would shake him. But in the end they remained silent.

In the long silence Pilate studied the Galilean, and though, as I have said, he had at another time questioned him at length, he still looked at him with the curiosity he would have for an utter stranger. "Hear me," he said suddenly. "Do you really think you are the Son of God?"

"If you say so."

"It's not what I say," Pilate said patiently. "Have you been saying this?"

"You have heard them. No one will say he heard me say these things. But I am the truth."

"Yes," Pilate said, smiling for the first time. "But what is truth?"

Before he could answer, the officer standing behind Pilate bent down, and Pilate turned to listen. I had quickened, expecting to be amused by the Galilean's answer to the philosophical question. Years later I found myself wishing he had answered. I would have known so much more about him.

Turning again to the Galilean, Pilate said, "They say

you call yourself King of the Jews. Are you King of the Jews?"

The man in the brown coat answered, "My kingdom is not of this world."

All the Romans present had been waiting for a chance to laugh at the Galilean and the priests. The whole examination was simply another Jewish comedy to them. The Galilean's answer delighted them. They were all grinning. One burst out laughing. Pilate made an abrupt motion with his hand. The soldier was quickly hustled out of the hall.

Pilate went back to pondering over the answer. We all waited, smiling. Then, astonishing me, he nodded sympathetically, as if he understood the Galilean's answer. I thought of Pilate's wife. In the way her hand had come out to him when he showed he was troubled, she had revealed she knew he had an inner world where all his real defeats and real triumphs took place. Here in his high place he now looked very lonely. What a strange man he was. The Roman policy! The grip of the Roman policy. Policy was his destiny. I didn't know what he could do.

"The charges against this man," he began, then, eyeing the priest, he paused, tapping the tips of his fingers on the arm of the chair, tapping and tapping. Suddenly straightening up, his whole manner changed as if he had found a dignified way out, and he stepped down from the dais. Without even turning to the officer standing behind him he walked toward the door. His officers immediately followed him. I joined them. The two guards took hold of the Galilean and dragged him along.

When he was on the railed balcony overlooking the courtyard Pilate raised his arm, remaining motionless for a full minute while the crowd shouted. Then, with a grand imperial gesture, he asked for silence. He held on to the long silence, waiting. Then suddenly he cried out that he had a gift for them. In the tradition of the Passover feast a prisoner was to be given his freedom. If it was their will, this king of the Jews, and he pointed at the Galilean, would be given his freedom now.

"No! Not him! Not him!" The chorus of angry voices, and the determination in the voices, seemed to stun Pilate. He stood still, looking over those fierce faces. I don't know why he referred to the Galilean as the King of the Jews, unless his mind had taken a jesting twist, or unless he hoped to touch some sense of humor in the crowd. But where were the Galilean's followers? Where were the poor and the dispossessed? Or were they too frightened to come to the courtyard? Not one voice cried out, "Yes, free the Galilean." It was as if they were all completely unaware of what that poor man in the brown coat might do for them if he could have his way.

And then my heart took a leap: Simon, I thought of Simon. I whispered his name, waiting to hear it shouted. Then into the hullabaloo came a lone voice I recognized, John of Jericho yelling, "Free Simon the Idumaean," then another voice shouting, "Free Simon." It was Isaiah. And these two voices so moved me I could have wept, and I tensed, waiting to hear the cry taken up. What did I care about the Galilean?

But other voices now were chanting. "Free Barabbas! Barabbas! Barabbas!" Who was this Barabbas? I was stunned. As the chant became a roar, I felt a chill around my heart, then a horror of myself. I knew I should have fixed it. I could have bought a hundred voices chanting Simon's name. Any money I had left — the money

Simon's wife had — whatever hidden loot there was — I should have given to John of Jericho to recruit the voices. My incompetence bewildered me. I came from a world where mourners were paid to attend funerals. What had dulled my wits? What stuff in the back of my mind had distracted me? Judas!

In one great voice the crowd roared "Barabbas! Barabbas!" until, raising his arm, Pilate said, "Very well, free this Barabbas," and wheeling around, he left the balcony. We followed him back to the judgment hall.

I couldn't take my eyes off Pilate. Instead of taking his place on the dais, he began to pace up and down in front of his judgment seat, pausing sometimes, his face gloomy, then taking up the slow march, then pausing again as if something held him rapt. Suddenly he turned to face the Galilean, trying to meet his eyes, seeking a consoling recognition of what was in his own mind, and he waited, and waited. Then, getting no recognition, he shouted angrily, "Then scourge him, scourge him here."

The three soldiers who were to handle the scourging left the hall, and while they were gone the Galilean, a soldier on each side of him, seemed perplexed, as if he hadn't foreseen the changing moods of Pilate and the troubled interventions. Yet their eyes had met. In a long silence their eyes had met, and they must have known each other in the silence, and yet they had said nothing.

When the three soldiers returned with thick sticks, the two who were guarding Jesus retired. The three, taking over, tried to turn the abuse into a comic thing, since they were now free to have some brutal fun. The moon-faced one with the wide mouth and the bad teeth slapped Jesus hard across the face, then with a laugh pushed him at the stocky soldier with the graying hair, who in turn slapped him and pushed him at the third soldier, who got in his slap. This third soldier, tall, thin, and blank-eyed, never stopped grinning. They kept up the pushing and slapping till the Galilean, stumbling, fell to the ground, moaning. Then they beat him with their sticks.

Oh, Pilate could be cruel, when he thought he had to be cruel. But he had never given me the impression that he enjoyed cruelty, and I didn't know what he was doing now — unless he was taking out his frustration with this scourging.

I had seen many men being beaten, some who suffered defiantly, their shrieks of pain telling of their defiance and courage, and others who literally squealed for mercy. But there was something new and terrible in this poor wretch's moans. If he had closed his eyes when he moaned — but he didn't; and in the eyes was acceptance — acceptance of the blows and the suffering. Was he mad, quite as mad as that Alexandrian magician? If he had any magic at all, why couldn't he stop this beating?

Then suddenly I was frightened. Judas had said it. This could be like the night when Judas had led the Sanhedrin men to Jesus. According to Judas, everybody had behaved as if they had been put under a spell. The disciples had dumbly fled. Judas had felt they were all behaving as if they were in a ritual dance. Now the moans of the poor man, whose brown coat had now been slashed as the heavy sticks rose and fell, told of his acceptance of things that had been written. Was this his magic? Making them all act out a story? All but Pilate, who, still trying to get out of the pattern, turned away, holding himself and waiting — for what? Coming to myself, angry and rational again, I thought, all this silly talk in Jerusalem about "as it was written." Too much poring over the meaning of the word, the meaning of the meaning, then the meaning behind the meaning. When I hear someone say "as it was written," I say cynically, "Well, who wrote it and why?"

Pilate said suddenly, "Enough. It's enough," and the soldiers dragged the Galilean to his feet, two of them supporting him, for he no longer had the strength to stand. Pilate, calling the third one, gave him some instructions and the soldier hurried from the hall. The Galilean, who had closed his eyes as they picked him up, swayed, straightened, opened his eyes, and looked around with an unbearable calm, as if he had easily put aside his suffering, and the officers sitting near me whispered in admiration.

Then the soldier, returning with a red cloak and a silly crown of some kind, clapped the silly crown on the head of the Galilean, laughing as he did so, and draped the cloak over his shoulders.

When this had been done, Pilate gave a signal, and the officers, I among them, followed him out to the balcony. When he had Jesus stand beside him the crowd roared approval. They could see that the Galilean, badly beaten, was there in a clown's costume that mocked him as a king.

Looking out over the lifted faces, the faces so full of life, satisfaction, and anticipation, I knew I had always hated an exultant crowd whether in Rome or Damascus or here in Jerusalem. An exultant crowd has just one face. Soon they have only one voice.

After asking for silence, Pilate cried in a loud voice, "Look upon this man — and yet I have found nothing against him — nothing," and now, a catch in my throat, I knew why Pilate had ordered the scourging. This man he had found nothing against stood there with bruises and blood from the beating on his face, his hair dishevelled, the silly crown askew on his head, beaten, humiliated, degraded, exhibited there for further mockery, and I was sure — oh, I was so certain Pilate believed that the crowd, having been told he judged no crime had been committed by the Galilean, would cry out in some natural sense of justice, or even in some compassion, "It is enough. Look at him. Let him go."

Pilate was making a terrible mistake; I saw it and wanted to cry out. He was counting on the crowd's sense of justice and compassion. Now, letting them look at Jesus in his abject state, Pilate waited for them to turn away, satisfied. But when there were only more mocking cries, he whispered to an officer, who left the balcony. The mocking cries continued till the officer returned with a basin of water. Having the officer hold the basin, Pilate dipped his hands in the water, and washed them, while a wondering silence fell on the crowd. And he cried, "I wash my hands of this innocent man. Look at him. Now what more do you want to do with him?"

In the terrible silence they all looked at the bound, ridiculous figure whose head was not bowed, and someone screeched, "Crucify him." Soon they were all chanting, "Crucify him."

Pilate's plan had failed. His mistake was that he did not see that this crowd of Jews was now just another crowd, and a crowd has no compassion when a beaten, humiliated, and degraded man is shown to them; they hate him for getting himself into this shameful position which is a humiliation to all of them, and they want to kill him. The chant continued, louder and more insistent. "Then let him be crucified," Pilate said, and quickly left the balcony. He was going to his apartment. I got in his way and he saw me. "I forgot they're not like us," he said.

I don't know whether or not Pilate felt that, in giving in, he had betrayed himself. Washing his hands of it as he did, was he making a desperate gesture to his conscience? I don't know. A little later that day I heard he had given instructions that a sign with the words "King of the Jews" should be nailed to the cross. The priests tried to persuade him to change the lettering to "He called himself King of the Jews." But since the crucifixion was now a Roman business, maybe Pilate took a savage and mocking satisfaction in having his way in this small matter. I don't know. Pilate troubled me; he moves my heart to this day. Later on, much later on, when there was trouble in Samaria and he slaughtered so many Samarians that he was recalled to Rome, I thought I knew what had happened to him.

It had been a terrible afternoon for him, this trial, and at the end just as terrible for me. Before leaving the Antonia I learned that Simon was to be crucified at the same time as the Galilean, and I wanted to be alone and weep.

XVI

If my presence at Simon's execution should be noted with surprise by Roman soldiers, I was prepared to say that Pilate himself might want a record of what happened, especially if a riot followed the Galilean's death. But fundamentally I didn't care what anyone said. I felt driven to have Simon recognize me, to see me there at his side and know he would remain in my heart forever. I kept seeing him as he had been that first night in the Judean hills just before accepting me as a friend and partner. I kept seeing him crouched on the ground, staring into the midnight sky, intent on reading the flickering motions of some one star that told him about the course of his life, and how I was to be thrust into it. I remembered, too, how strangely exciting and new he seemed, free from his tribal god and the tribal laws. But free as he was, in his soul he knew that one star, acting upon him, made him what he was. I was sure something of me was in Simon, something recklessly adventurous, but always half hidden in me. Oh, I liked him, I liked being with him, and if he crossed the river now, then I, too, one day would cross the same river. But if death was to be just a long sleep for him, so it would be for me too. And is there anything as refreshing as a long, untroubled sleep? But if we are to waken at the end of the sleep, then we are in the world of Orpheus and the heroes, and how could Simon or any man ask for more? Oh, noble thoughts, broken-hearted noble thoughts, with which a man buoys himself up when a good friend is leaving this earth and the arms of his young wife.

On this day of the execution, a cloudy sunless windy day with the gritty desert dust blowing over city streets, I was glad to hear that Simon and another thief had been taken in a wagon to Golgotha, the execution place of the skulls, outside the city walls and on a low hill near a cemetery and a garden. I saw only a part of the Galilean's march through the streets, dragging his cross halfway across the city. Staggering along in his brown coat, he had his arms curled up over the crossbar, apparently heedless of the mocking cries coming from crowds lining the streets. Looking back now, I can't remember the faces, any faces in the crowd, only the hats, the long row of brightly colored turbans. Crowds, yes, but there were gaps in the line of the hats, places where no one had stayed to watch, perhaps having been shamed away, which I understood, too. For as that poor man in the brown coat stumbled along, sometimes falling on the stones under the weight of the cross, I felt suddenly as if everyone I knew was staggering, falling, and trembling too. I had never had such a feeling.

His face showed all the misery and desolation he had been able to hide at the trial. Oh, I pitied him, not just for

this suffering, but for being in the grip of all those
fantasies that had put him here, that had even convinced
him that he could raise the temple. Yet now, falling, he
could not even lift his cross. As a man jumped out of the
crowd to help him, I saw the Galilean's tears. If Judas was
there in the crowd what would he say now about the
poor man asking for all this suffering? Was this how he
had his way with death? Could Judas, watching, believe
his own story now?

Even in the animal world, I have noticed, a killing
action that goes too far is resented. Animals back away,
unless they are very hungry. The Romans now were
going too far, humiliating and torturing the Galilean.
Pilate himself had gone too far, ordering this public
parade of the man's torment. Well, I pitied Pilate, I pitied
him as much as I pitied the poor broken man in the
brown coat. He had not only given in; resenting his
inner defeat, he had gone savagely the other way. Policy?
Well, in the name of policy he would give these people
even more than they were entitled to ask, even more
than they could stomach, more than they could ever
bear to remember.

Yes, Pilate moved me and I think he may indeed have
moved the man in the brown coat. Surely the Galilean
would understand, if he was as wise and uncannily
perceptive as Judas said, that Pilate was unfortunate
enough to have an inner domain and had been unable to
defend it. If Pilate had been emperor and had all the
power, he would have been a rare just man, and I
wouldn't have been here watching. Wherever Pilate and
his troubled wife went now he could go on wearing his
blue cloak, he could wear out hundreds of blue cloaks,

but the blue of Aphrodite could not ward off the pursuing furies, nor could the correct and brutal policy, the
things he kept on doing.

Having had enough of the street display of the poor
Messiah's misery, I hurried to a tavern to have a drink. In
the tavern someone spoke to me, but I heard only the
beating of my own heart. I did not want to hear anything
else.

An hour later when I made my way to the place of
skulls, the street seemed to have been cleared of the
crowd, and I wondered if all of them, in violation of their
custom, had hurried beyond the gate to the site of execution so they could taunt the Galilean on his cross. It was
late in the afternoon, and there were deep wheel ruts in
the road up the hill. There was more wind now, more
dust, and the sky had darkened when I reached the place.
There was no crowd. So few had come I felt conspicuous,
wondering what I could say if asked what was my business there.

Just to the right, on the hill's rim, were two men and a
woman in a wagon with big wheels, well back, as if in
their wagon they could fade suddenly over the rim and
be gone, and working on the crosses on the ground were
twelve Roman soldiers. Six others watched the three
figures being stretched on the crosses. Near by were two
women, one of them much younger than the other,
accompanied by a young man. The two women were
holding each other and weeping, and I could have wept
myself as I heard the hammer's heavy blows driving the
nails into wrists and feet. Blood spurted as the nails sank
in. I couldn't distinguish Simon's cries and moans from
those of the other thief and the Galilean.

Those kneeling Romans, busy with their hammers

and nails, were as efficient as workmen on a bridge, and so competent they could joke with each other while working. When the nailing was done, all the Romans lent a hand in raising the first cross and sinking the shaft into the hole they had dug, then packing the loose earth around it. It was the cross of the Galilean. Now that he was upright, blood from his wounds streamed down his limbs. He had been stripped of his coat, the brown coat tossed aside as if it might have some value and be worth taking away. On the cross the Galilean had only a loin-cloth, but the soldiers, paying special attention to him, had put on a crown of thorns on his head, and above the crown, nailed to the cross, a parchment with the large lettering "The King of the Jews." There it was. Pilate's small bitter mocking satisfaction. I went closer so that I could read the lettering.

They raised the cross of the second thief, whose name I did not know, then Simon's, and as his cross was thrust against the skyline, such a tightness came in my chest and throat that I thought I would stifle. "Simon, Simon," I finally whispered, begging him with all my heart to turn his head to me. No cries came from the three on their crosses; if they were moaning I could not hear the moans. The soldiers sat down to watch and wait, although what they were waiting for I didn't know, unless it was nightfall, or the final death cries. As the head of the Galilean sank to his chest and his eyes closed, the two women and the young man moved closer to his cross, and when the soldiers did not object, the young man looked up at the Galilean and spoke and kept on speaking till the Galilean spoke to him. I did not hear what was said. Anyway, I was watching Simon, who, having opened his eyes as if he had mastered his pain, turned his head so he could see the rim of the low bare hill, and his eyes remained fixed on those three distant figures in the wagon. In the wagon the young woman had seen him turn his head, and as Simon cried out in a language I could not understand, she knelt in the wagon, her arms raised to him.

I kept moving around, in the hope that any figure moving on this bare hill would attract Simon's attention, and at last he saw me; his eyes remained on me. As I slowly raised my hand, and he smiled, I felt such a tremendous relief: the beautiful recognition, the meeting, then the parting. But the stillness in the air was broken by a sudden gust of wind so cold it made me shiver, and it swept the Roman officer's cloak wide, away from his shoulders, holding it out like wide flapping crimson wings, his helmet a beak between them, then the wings flapped back around his neck, covering his face, and the air was still again.

The Galilean had turned his head to console the thief whose name I did not know. This thief was alone, not one friend had come there — I did not even know who he was. I think the Galilean was telling him he was not alone now. Then Simon, in his turn, spoke to the Galilean, and as they exchanged a few words I felt something like a chill, no, a kind of uneasy wondering awareness that these two men, who had come into my life at about the same time, and kept coming in, though they had never met, at last were speaking, having come to this place to die together.

The Galilean had enough strength left to speak to the three who stood near his cross, the young man and the two women, and I heard the word "Mother?" which meant the other weeping woman was his own mother

— I could not see her face. On hearing the Galilean's words the young man put his arm protectively around the older woman, a gesture which must have been meant that from now on he would look after her. I thought the young man must have been the Galilean's brother.

While these things were being done, the soldiers sat around in a circle, amusing themselves as if nothing had happened here they hadn't seen a hundred times in places stretching from Parthia to Gaul. Their talk and laughter were the only sounds on that desolate hill till a bird, a lone bird of the twilight, began to sing. Those three figures in the big wheeled wagon on the rim of the hill, Simon's wife, Isaiah, and John, were standing, utterly motionless, watching, waiting for Simon to turn his head once more. But then Simon's body, losing all tension in the limbs, went slack; and as the chin dropped, there was a terrible wrench at my heart, then leaden loneliness.

All day the sky had been gray and by this time, with all light fading, the streams of blood on the limbs of the three on their crosses were just long black streaks, and I could no longer read the lettering "King of the Jews" over the mocking crown of thorns. The Galilean's mother sobbed. The young man stared up at the Galilean, who moaned. He wanted water. One of the soldiers, jumping to his feet almost exuberantly, dipped a sponge in a pail, and putting it on the end of a spear, thrust it against the Galilean's mouth, tormenting him till one of his comrades, who had picked up the brown coat, called out; putting down the sponge and the spear, he came and examined the coat. They all took turns evaluating the garment. The one who had first picked it up began to claim it. Then suddenly he stiffened, so startled that he dropped the coat, as the Galilean uttered a loud cry. I have never heard such a loud heartbroken cry of utter loneliness, and I shuddered. Never in my life have I felt so lonely, or been in a place so desolate as this place in the deepening darkness.

One of the soldiers, jumping up, shook his head; he had had enough of this. He was a thick-shouldered bowlegged man. Taking his spear, he approached the Galilean, his step in the approach tentative, almost gentle. And then suddenly he thrust the spear deep into his side, and put him out of his misery. Throwing down the spear, he made an angry gesture at the soldier who had tormented the Galilean with the sponge.

Rooted there, I took a last long look at Simon's great bearded face, now fallen forward. The young man, his arm around the weeping mother, came my way, and as they passed, the younger woman said to me, "Are you one of us? You must be."

I told her I was a friend of Mary of Samaria. "I saw you in the parade," I said. "You're Mary of Magdalene," and I bowed, profoundly moved by the mixture of sensuality and suffering in her face.

"I know Pilate would have had it otherwise," I said.

"It doesn't matter," she said.

"Where are the others? The men so close to him?"

"They have things to do."

"Oh, I'm sure they have," I said cynically, since Judas had told me they had all fled when the Galilean had been seized. I assumed they were afraid they would be arrested if they showed themselves here. Or were they like those Canaanites, squatting round the fire in their courtyard, waiting to see if he could do what he said he could do? But with a glance I could not fathom she said apologetically, "The burial has to be arranged. The cemetery is near by," and turned to leave.

After taking a few steps she turned again to take a last look at this bare place, at the leaden sky where two birds circled, then circled again, and she seemed to be listening. While she listened she began to weep. The tears told me that even if she believed her Galilean could do what he said he would, she was enough of a woman to fear that she might never walk with him again, never see the sunlight on his face again, or feel the wind blowing against them in the hills.

As my heart went out to her, I could see her as she had been in the parade, serene and smiling; Judas, too, in that parade, marching along in his fine robe and expensive turban, all by himself with his princely air. Walking beside her mounted king, she suddenly looked up at him. They spoke, and as the others started to sing, tossing out flowers from baskets on their arms, she laughed out loud, such a warm earth-loving laugh. Some of them started to dance, and as they came dancing by, Judas, seeing me, beckoned and pointed, asking me to follow. I had waited, and yet I had followed the parade to its end here. Outside the desert all of Judea was a beautiful garden at this time of the year, a gay flower bed, yet they had been parading up to this one desolate spot where she now stood listening — listening as if the despairing cry of her dying lover was still on the bleak wind.

"I must go," she said abruptly, and leaving me, she hurried to catch up to her friends. I followed her with my eyes, and when she vanished I grew agitated. Never had I felt so lonely and discontented. I wanted to get far away. If only I could find some secret magic place where my life would be all bright new things, I thought. Then I had a strange flight of fancy. I saw myself in Alexandria, Rome, Athens, the islands, seeking the one right secret place; then, tiring of the search, I turned, looking back, and in my daydream I saw her watching me, smiling faintly. But harsh cries from those two circling birds broke my fancy. I felt a chill. The twilight was deepening. On my way down the low slope I saw that the three who had remained on the rim of the hill, Simon's wife, Isaiah, and John, were now heading for their wagon, and were deliberately changing direction so they could pass close by. Coming no closer than three feet, they did not even turn their heads, so no Roman soldier watching would believe they offered me recognition. As they passed, Isaiah, the one closest to me, said out of the corner of his mouth, "Be at the inn tomorrow — before noon."

"What for?" I asked.

"Simon's wife has nothing now."

"I'm sorry."

"Come up with something, Philo. Some rich merchant on the road. Tomorrow. Understand?" and they passed on, leaving me angered by the words. With Simon gone and his loyalty to me gone, too, a loyalty which Isaiah had felt compelled to share to some extent, he wouldn't hesitate now to betray me to the Romans for money.

Turning, I looked back at those crosses on the hill and at the soldiers who were now picking up their weapons. Then, hurrying away down the hill, I began to feel amazingly hungry, even greedy, greedy for wine and the sight of young girls whirling in a wild dance. In Jerusalem, which is a priest-dominated, essentially Jewish city, you can, nevertheless, get anything you want, for in the city are little pockets of other peoples, pretending to be

Jews, who have strange and ancient gods they serve in ways that are not Jewish, but come from long before this Jewish time. And I knew a place where there was always wild music and Dionysian girls who became part of the music.

Two hours later I went to Ezekiel's house, where I could be sure of good company, good food, and good wine.

XVII

My physician's house had a lovely garden with hanging lanterns, and coming to the house by way of the garden, I found four of the young wives sitting there gossiping. The weather had changed. The low gray clouds of the afternoon had been broken up by the wind, which had died down by nightfall, and now there was a moon and stars and a warm softness in the garden air. From the house came the sound of men's voices raised in heated discussion, the sound, too, of the harp, and I imagined that Mordechai with the delicate hands was playing for himself while the others argued.

The wives begged me to sit with them for a few minutes and tell what had been going on. In the lantern light their pretty faces were like bright blooms on the thick heavy plants behind them. Their jewels glittered in the lamplight, and they all wore headbands. One had a ring at her nose, and when an arm moved, a bangle tinkled, the sound making the garden seem even more opulent. I liked the oriental opulence of rich Jews, I liked the ease of their women with a man they knew liked women, which I have always done. Wherever I am, women talk to me, and I learn more about what is really going on from their gossipy kind of conversation than I do from the direct information I get from men. Women have a more personal awareness, and their own kind of logic, which is often like the leapfrogging logic of a dream.

That pretty girl from Tyre, married to the elderly rich merchant, said, "You meet everyone, Philo. You must have met this Galilean. What was he like?"

"A young man in a brown coat. He looked like a poet. I saw the execution."

"You saw it? What were you doing there? No one goes there."

"To record it — for Pilate. It was horrible."

"No one goes to these executions. I don't want to hear about it."

"Yes, it was horrible," I said again, then I couldn't give in and drop it. "After a while he hung there silent — for a long time, and then suddenly, after one terrible piercing shriek at the heavens, he died. It was the loneliest cry I have ever heard."

The ladies said nothing. Nor did I break the silence. They no longer wanted me there with them.

Then there was the sound of the harp from the house, a sound I have always loved. How beautiful this garden and those shadowed flower faces seemed after that bare hill, and now there was the lovely sound of the harp.

"Philo, Philo — are you there?" Ezekiel called from the house. Taking my arm, he led me into the large room and past the group still arguing among themselves. Some of them I did not know, but Mordechai with the elegant hands was there, which meant that someone else, a paid musician, played the harp in an adjoining room. I knew the others here: the elderly aristocratic rich merchant with the long white beard and the childlike wife, and the two higher priests, Eleazar and Phineas. Guiding me past them to the table heaped with viands and wine jars, Ezekiel, heaping food on my plate, said, "You know Pilate, don't you, Philo? You see him?" Gulping my food greedily, I answered that Pilate saw me only when he wanted to see me. But yes, I knew his moods and his temperament. Why?

At the sound of Pilate's name, and as if they had been waiting, the others gathered around. I kept on eating, saying not a word. The others listened to the physician, their grave bearded faces full of concern, nodding as he said he was sure I had heard the word being spread all over the city, that the dead Galilean would rise on the third day and show himself. Well, this was nonsense, of course, and something to be laughed at, and yet who was spreading the story? And why? The council knew that the Galilean's followers had begun to disperse as soon as they had heard he had been seized, running off into the country, or going into hiding; and now that the blasphemer had been executed there was every evidence that his following would vanish completely, soon be forgotten.

Yet someone was bent on bringing them all together again. It was possible that the Galilean himself, driven half mad by wild dreams of power, had issued instructions before he had been seized. What if his followers had an incredible piece of trickery in mind, something to dazzle his disappointed and disillusioned illiterate followers — something to bring them swarming in from miles away, believing pathetically that the Galilean had the magic of the Son of God, and crying out against his executioners? They might riot, they might burn. But if they were to become a rebellious multitude again, they needed some proof of magic. So what if they had a young man who looked like Jesus, who could be made to look even more like him, then . . .

I had finished eating, but since I had heard all this before, I wondered what they wanted of me, and as my mind started to wander, I though of Simon. Not one word here about Simon! And oh, how these people loved to exaggerate. People of the exaggerated word they call the law. Yes, Ezekiel went on, some Sanhedrin members, having heard stories about the Galilean's promise to appear again, recognized that they should have asked Pilate to allow them to take possession of the body and bury it in a secret place. Caiaphas himself was prepared to go to Pilate, until, just an hour ago, word came that Joseph of Arimathea, hurrying to Pilate, had received permission to place the body in a new tomb he owned in the nearby cemetery. Already there had been a hasty burial.

Alert now, I said, "Joseph of Arimathea!" and they nodded, some scowling. One aristocratic old man, his eyes hard, was clenching and unclenching his old hands, and they all looked very hurt and betrayed. Joseph. Why Joseph? I had met him, a rich middle-aged merchant who lived with his two daughters in a house near by; the house had a beautiful garden with ponds and bronze figures as in the ponds in Herod's palace, for Joseph, too, liked the Greek influence. But Joseph was an esteemed member of the community who sacrificed in the temple. And being rich, too, he could not possibly want to be stripped of his riches. How could such a man intervene now? Unless out of sheer pity for the Galilean, whom he might have seen suffering on the street, a man without a friend, a degraded young Jew going to an unmarked grave. In his rich independence, Joseph might have decided that he agreed with Pilate; Jesus was a just man, unjustly killed.

Then my physician, turning, explained that they were sharing their alarm because I could be of some help. Since I knew Pilate I could give them advice. Would it be wise of them, he wanted to know, to hurry to Pilate now, to tell him they had got word of some planned trickery, and ask for his permission to take over the body, since Jesus had been a Jew, and give it a deep burial of their own?

I said quickly and in all honesty that I thought they would be inviting trouble which might lead to insult and a very serious situation. They would be going too far. Everybody had been going too far. Already Pilate felt they had had their way with him, and wouldn't give an inch where he didn't have to. In my opinion, I said, they should leave Pilate out of it. Do what they wanted to do — but do it by themselves.

While they were all reluctantly agreeing with me the ladies came in from the garden, bringing conversation, laughter, and more wine, all of which began to fray my nerves. The whole day had shattered me. When I stared resentfully at a pretty woman who kept smiling at me, she grew upset, and I knew I should be home in bed.

As soon as I was on the street my imagination began to race wildly. Who had gone so quickly to Joseph of Arimathea? Mary Magdalene? Ah, she could move him. She could get any man to do her bidding, and she would be the one to know if Joseph was a secret sympathizer. Yet aside from her, the Galilean's followers, underground now for days, might indeed be well organized, and I remembered those three I had seen furtively hurrying away from the house of Mary of Samaria. All kinds of thoughts whirled through my tired-out mind. I even wondered where that brown coat was.

In my room I flopped on the bed, but as soon as I closed my eyes I saw Simon's face. I saw him talking to Jesus, and they talked, and kept talking, like old comrades; and though I strained to hear, knowing that what was being said was important and should be remembered, I couldn't hear a word.

My troubled sleep gave me no rest, and in the morning I had to drag myself up the hill to the Antonia to see if my services were required in any capacity. I trudged along in that cruel hard sunlight, that slashing sunlight peculiar to this land. At the Antonia I tried talking casually to officers about the executions. They remained detached, uninvolved; the job had been done. And as for the Galilean's painful march through the streets, one officer said with a shrug, "These things happen in this kind of a country."

Later I saw Felix, Pilate's attendant, and chatted amiably with him. I said I'd been hoping Pilate might have asked for me. Felix told me the procurator had shut himself off in his apartment with his wife; and yet — and this was interesting — Felix said Pilate had consented to see Jospeh of Arimathea, who had come rushing to him early last evening, saying he had got word the priests planned to take possession of the Galilean's body before a place could be found for a burial, and before any great gathering could mourn him. It seemed to Felix that

Pilate had a sympathetic interest in Joseph's story, even drawing him aside, talking quietly, sharing a troubled concern, and Felix had heard Pilate say, parting from Joseph, "He's dead. Can't they understand? — he's dead. Can't these fanatical priests leave him alone, even though he's dead? How far do they want to go?"

I got away quickly from the fortress so I could go home and pray for some real sleep that would rid me of the drowsy numbness in my brain. And as soon as I got home I did fall into a heavy sleep, but I had wild dreams. Now dreams, though very important, are dangerous in the divinations they offer, as dangerous as the advice from those oracles whose foreseeing wisdom has to be interpreted properly. I have learned to avoid delving too deeply into my own dreams for divinations, unless the dream is so vivid that it wakes me suddenly, my heart beating unsteadily. I have always put more reliance on those faint interior whispers you can hear on the border-line between sleep and wakefulness, although even here there is a danger. For if you concentrate too intently, listening, you hear too many whispers — a rapid flow of whispers, taking over, and leaving you no mind of your own. It can be frightening. Yet I know powerful men in Rome who are guided in all their actions by interior whispers they have caught at the right time. As for where these whispers come from, it may be that in the underworld there are thousands of guides trying to get at you, as there may be a hundred gods wanting your veneration. But as I say, I fell sound asleep before I could ask a question and listen for a whispered answer.

In my dream I was fifteen years old again in Crete, and swimming far out in the heavy wine-dark sea, and suddenly the sea changed, I was in trouble, I was drowning; I cried out, and a dolphin took care of me, pushing me towards the shore. Then, as it happens in dreams where time has no meaning, I was as old as I am now, and mounted on a beautiful white stallion, racing trium-phantly along a wide white beach, exulting in the speed and power of my godlike horse, till suddenly, just ahead, was a wall of darkness, a heavy blob with the center of darkness shifting, and full of mad shadows. The awful shadows didn't frighten me. Shouting exultantly, I urged the horse on, sending the white beast hurtling through the dancing deep shadows to the light ahead. But the stallion, rearing back, neighed angrily, and neighed again, pawing furiously at the sand.

The pawing became a pounding, a knocking, and I jumped up, not sure I was awake, for a wild face belong-ing to the dream came at me. A figure in the doorway had pushed the door open after knocking; the door was still swinging. As the figure came into the light from the window, I saw it was Judas Iscariot, staring at me, his face deathly pale; and the mixture of wild hope and utter despair in the face frightened me.

XVIII

The last time I had seen him he had been dishevelled, with bruises on his face from stones thrown at him, but even so there had been pride in him, his eyes shining with crazy excitement, some sense of glory he got out of enduring humiliations for the sake of someone he loved. There was no pride left in him now. And what was this? A brown coat. He was wearing a brown coat. Shaken, I went closer. It wasn't the brown coat, and I was relieved.

"What do you want, Judas?" I asked.

"Just a few words," he said, coming in and slumping in a chair like a man so badly beaten he was close to death. I thought he was suffering remorse, even though he had seemed to believe that the Galilean had needed him. But he had seen what it had come to, he had seen the Galilean in agony in the streets on the way to his death. Knowing he had had a hand in it, I thought, had finally overwhelmed him.

"You saw him, I take it," I said, shrugging.

"I saw him, yes," he whispered. "No, I only half saw him, my eyes were too full of tears. Even though it was as he said it would be, as he wanted it to be, the pain of seeing it was terrible but . . ."

"But what, Judas?"

"Philo," he blurted out. "My story . . . I don't want it done. I'm not going to pay you. Just forget it."

"That's all right for you, Judas, but I've taken notes. If I don't write it out now, I've wasted my time."

"You have the notes here, Philo?"

"I have the notes. Yes."

"Give them back to me."

"What for, Judas? What do you want to do?"

"Tear them up. Throw them away. Burn them."

"And my work goes for nothing? Well, I don't know. I'll think about it."

"I told you to give them to me, Philo," he hissed, but his sudden anger turned me against him. "Give them to me," he said, his voice rising as he looked at my desk, looking for the notes that weren't there, but were out of sight in the drawer. The swing of his head was so frantic and despairing as he looked around that I wanted to back away, fearing he might have gone mad from remorse. Then his eyes, meeting mine, told me he was not mad. He was trying desperately to believe that if he had the notes he would be safe. Safe from what? From someone pursuing him who must not know his story? I didn't know, and I grew bewildered. Grabbing his arm, I pointed to a chair. But he backed away. Then, reaching into his coat for his purse, he took out a handful of silver and tossed it on the desk. "There. See, Philo. I'll pay you for the notes. Isn't it enough? Here," and he took out another handful of silver. "Say what you want. Take it all. I'll burn the notes, and you can forget I ever came here. What about it?"

That silver on the desk made me uneasy. Then I shivered, and since I didn't know why I shivered, I was angry at myself for having any emotion about that money. Wanting to get rid of him quickly, I opened the desk drawer, took out the notes, and while he watched me, his eyes suddenly bright with hope or pain, I lit a candle and began to burn the notes. He watched the ashes drop to the floor and become a little pile.

My eyes were on the flame so it wouldn't burn my fingers, but I heard him sit down, breathing heavily, and then he sighed. I thought it was a deep sigh of relief, though it sounded more like a moan of a wounded animal, and I said gruffly, "There you are, Judas. I don't want your money," and I swept it from the desk to the floor. "But in view of all that's happened here, how can I forget your story?"

"Yes, the story," he whispered. "It's still there, isn't it?"

"I'd just as soon forget it, Judas."

"No, sooner or later you'll talk."

"I say I won't, Judas."

"It doesn't matter. As long as you're alive, it's there."

"Well, you could try and kill me."

"What good would it do? It's out now. It'll live. Sooner or later it will be told. And I knew it. I knew it," he whispered, "I saw it even while the notes burned."

Slumping deeper in the chair, he seemed to grow smaller under my eyes — a man shattered by terrible disappointment in himself. Then his tears! He let the tears fall and didn't care that they took away the last shreds of his self-esteem. Inert in that brown coat, he didn't care about anything. Shaken by his awful loneli-

ness, I said gently, "I think I understand, Judas. You saw
the tears of Jesus when he stumbled and fell and it broke
your heart, and you hated yourself for betraying him."

"You're a fool, Philo," he said lifelessly. "I didn't betray
him."

"You mean — the story you told me — it's the true
story?"

"Of course it is," he muttered impatiently. "Every
word of it is true. I only did his bidding. No matter how I
suffered I could console myself I was doing his bidding."

Studying his hands, he frowned, then put them up
against his temples, then looked at them again with
loathing. "Yes, you're a fool, Philo," and his voice rose.
"Sympathetic about the wrong things. Don't you understand anything? I told you things. Secret things between
me and Jesus. Things never to be known. I did my part
and did it with love, but God help me, there was to be
silence and mystery, and I broke the silence. I couldn't
keep quiet, I failed my own love, and I know why."

Slumping in the chair, he kept nodding to himself and I
could hardly hear him. "It was my pride," he said. "My
terrible pride."

With a bitter smile, and never moving his head or his
hands, taking his time as if each slow word had great
meaning for him, even though it tortured him — and it
did, his face showed it did — he told me that all along he
had known he was superior to the others, and had been
proud to be the one chosen for this thing. And when he
had done it and had seen the others running and hiding
and cursing him, and had found he could bear the shame
and suffering, he had exulted, believing Jesus was with
him. And his pride in his suffering grew, and he told
himself that some day people should get the true story

— the greatness of his love and his suffering. They would want to hear it. "I talked," he said, his voice sinking to a whisper, "I broke the silence."

"Just to me, Judas," I said soothingly.

Standing up, he faced me with a lonely tattered dignity, but then his shoulders shook, and, sobbing, he had to turn away. But he got control of himself. "Not tomorrow, or the next day, but on the third day Jesus will rise from the tomb, and be among us," he said quietly. "Do you think I can face him, Philo? No, I cannot face him."

"You can't?" and I blinked, confused. It was as if he had some way of knowing that the Galilean would appear, and he knew it as surely as he knew the sun would rise tomorrow; and this kind of knowledge, coming out of the mixture of love and despair in him, awed me, although I couldn't understand it.

"So I won't be here," he said quietly.

"Won't you?" I said, and began to pick up the silver and put it back in his coat pocket, while he watched motionless, his smile twisted. I told him I had to go out, and indeed it was true. Already I was late for my meeting with Isaiah. He could walk down the street with me, I said.

On the way down the street, the sound of his step put such a chill in me I suddenly revolted against it all: I laughed, I slapped his shoulder. I told him to come to his senses. Everyone around here now was going crazy, I said. It was about time everybody in this mad city came to their senses. And he should stop being such a credulous fool. It was madness to think he would have to face the Galilean in the streets of Jerusalem. The Galilean was dead. Good and dead. As dead as Simon, the Idumaean, who had died beside him. I had seen them die.

And life would go on without them, and he, like everyone
else in the world, would have to put up with the joys and
the sorrows and make the best of things as they are.

But he wouldn't even look at me. Even when we
parted he said nothing, and I shouted after him irritably,
"And throw away that damned coat."

XIX

I yelled at him because he offended me. He was a man who had intelligence, perception, and curiosity about the mystery of life and who should have been a poet, and look at him!

I went to the stables, got a horse, and rode out, Judas still on on my mind. But on a narrow street I was brought to a halt, the horse rearing. Ahead, a farmer's overloaded wagon had tilted, and three crates of chickens, falling in the street, had cracked open. Now twenty chickens were loose, clucking madly, half flying at the narrow street walls, being chased by a barking dog while the frantic farmer kicked at the dog, then chased the chickens, aided by three small boys, till the street folk made a circle, hemming the chickens in, and I, fuming, had to wait till the farmer cleared up the mess so I could get through and be off, with Judas back in my thoughts again.

This whole world of Judas, Jesus, and Jewish fantasy made me feel that I would suffocate if I didn't soon get out of it. Their demons and devils had got hold of all of them. Judas was no more obsessed than my good physician friend and those priests who were so wonderfully hospitable and full of music. Imagine, now they wanted to play games with a corpse — as if it were the new golden treasure. No wonder Simon preferred to be an outlaw. Knowing what he was, being what he was, and accepting his fate proudly without tears, he was superior to all of them. So let a great plague come and take the lot of them — they were all victims of this land, this center of hypnotic fantasies, whose people had been this way even before the tribes came. Indeed it might even be that seeds from some native plants, caught up in the desert wind, were still being blown across the land as they had been blown for thousands of years, making people insane: their whole history shaped by insanity. So if Mary of Samaria hated her own sensual loveliness — which had been so natural, and as surprisingly distinctive as those happy beautiful Thera paintings I had seen as a boy — why should I be surprised? Not so long ago in this land young men, devotees of Ishtar, used to castrate themselves so they could be faithful to her forever.

With the sky a fiery red in the west, I approached the gate, my eyes on all those towers on the wall and the stairs leading up to them. Towers against a blazing red sky, a city of towers keeping out the strangers' light. And I could see the temple, too. According to Judas, the Galilean had moved the temple out of Jerusalem; it was gone forever, moved into the hearts of men everywhere. Well, there it was — still there — oh, so very solidly there. I went on through the gate, trotting up the road to the inn, trying to put my mind on Isaiah. I hated having to come when that man called me. I had to get rid of him.

As soon as I entered the inn the shrewd-eyed bluff old innkeeper nodded, recognizing me, and pointed to a bench in a corner where Isaiah, sitting by himself, drank from a huge tankard. I was shocked that he should know that Isaiah had business with me. Never again would I meet Isaiah here — nor any other place, if I could only have my way. And I hated him for making it clear by his air that he was impatient at being kept waiting. I was his man in Jerusalem.

After Simon had been seized, Isaiah's whole manner had changed. He was leader now of a band of about sixteen, and everything about him had become bigger and uglier. His black beard had grown as long as Simon's, and his eyes, always full of conviction, were now bold and confident, as if he were sure that on his signal men would appear out of nowhere, ready to die for him. The fool actually believed this, though there was nothing in him but the brute strength in his big heavy shoulders and thick neck. There was nothing in his heart to gain anyone's loyalty; yet he thought he was now bigger than Simon because he was more ruthless, and therefore more to be feared. But his new sense of power only made him look even more like a thug — a thug in the clothes of a decent farmer. Sitting down on the bench beside him, I was sure the day would come when one of his own men would kill him, out of sheer resentment.

The corner where we sat was in heavy shadow. I couldn't see his face clearly, and I was glad. Yet I had to mollify him. Leaning closer with an air of suppressed excitement, I told him I had some information that would delight him. The prison captain who had made fools of us was leaving tomorrow morning with a troop of eight Romans to spend a week in Caesarea. I told him the road they would take. Then, pretending tense excitement, I whispered that while he and his band might be no match for the Romans, nevertheless an arrow from a hidden marksman, or better still a flight of arrows, then the marksmen vanishing . . . Even as I went on whispering, in my mind's eye I could see the Romans catching and killing Isaiah, hacking him to death.

"Good, good," he said with a distracted air, as if something more interesting than killing the captain was on his mind. Finally he said, "We buried Simon in that cemetery." But again he made me wait, wondering why he was grinning. Some travellers who came in were exchanging hearty greetings with the innkeeper, but Isaiah didn't turn; he kept his eyes on me, saying nothing. His eyes made me nervous. "So you buried Simon," I said, and his grin widening, he said, "Some of the Galilean's people were there. They've put him in a tomb, you know."

I can still remember Isaiah hunching his heavy shoulders and taking a big drink, wiping his mouth, then getting down to business. I can't remember his words, only the rough speech rhythms, and the rise and fall of his voice, but I can still see the white scar on his cheek. In the cemetery he and John looked like farmers, he said, and so they talked with the Galilean's people. At first there were only two women, and then others came to the tomb, many others, and they were all nervous, excited and half scared, too, about keeping the Galilean's body in the tomb. And so they had a very big stone rolled in front of the tomb, and now two women watched all night, leaving only when the stars faded and it got chilly. He and John had hung around in the morning, talking to them, wondering why they were all so concerned about guarding the body. What were they afraid of? And they learned that the Galilean was supposed to have had some magic, and they were all hoping — most of them just hoping — that he still had this magic, even though dead; and if he had it and showed it, their community wouldn't die. But they had got word that priests and Sanhedrin men would do anything to get possession of the body and bury it some place far away.

"I have heard these things," I said, filled with curiosity about his interest. And as I waited, and he let me wait, my inability to follow his thoughts further made him laugh. "You're a slow one, Philo," he said, beckoning to the innkeeper to bring him more wine. While he drank he said nothing more. Finally he said he had gone into the city at noon to loaf around the marketplace and the outer temple court and listen to the talk. There was talk, a lot of angry excited talk, about the Galilean in a fine tomb, and this talk was about some kind of a plot among the Galilean's followers to do something about the tomb, so that their movement wouldn't die, as it was already dying. Some said the council should order that the body should be taken away from the Galilean's followers, and taken at once and at any cost. And if the Sanhedrin wouldn't have this done, someone else should do it.

"So what do you say to this, Philo?" he asked.

"I've heard all this."

"It's not what I'd say," he said smugly. "I'd say that body is very, very valuable."

"You're mad too, Isaiah."

"Who else is mad?"

"You're all mad."

"They're all crazy about this thing. I know they're crazy. But see — that's good — because I'm not crazy."

Then he told me he had made a plan to take the body from the tomb and hide it; and then for a very large sum, a fortune, he said, he would let the Galilean's followers, or the Sanhedrin men, the highest bidder, take possession. The bad thing was, he said, that the Galilean's followers had no money.

Though stunned, or revolted, I heard myself saying, "Joseph of Arimathea is a very rich man. But the Romans will kill you." He shrugged. "The Romans want to kill me anyway. They killed Simon."

I stared at him for a long time; the mood of disgust with the warring wild fantasies of these people that I felt must have been touched, and I knew that if I were standing apart, and had heard that the thing Isaiah planned had actually happened, I would get a savage satisfaction out of it. I thought that Pilate himself, knowing that both the council men and the Galilean's followers were planning to use the poor Galilean's death for their own ends, might also get some satisfaction out of their bewilderment and dismay, and I said, "Why do you tell this to me? What's in it for me?"

XX

Before he could answer I said uneasily, "I want no part of this." And Isaiah, eyeing me, his face hardening, said I didn't have much choice, and I hated him. I had to be their man in Jerusalem, he said, and as far as he was concerned, I still was their man, and so would say the Romans. And besides, since I knew of the plan, he might have to kill me for his own protection. But why look for trouble? I had had no difficulty acting as a go-between, giving the bribe to the prison captain, who was out of the way now, as I said, on the road to Caesarea, and by nightfall he could have an arrow in his heart. My job as the go-between here should be an easy one. Not only did I know the rich man, Joseph of Arimathea, I also knew the Sanhedrin men. I had many Jewish friends who would readily believe that I was a likely man to have been approached as a go-between.

To this day my attitude to Isaiah fascinates me. While hating him for counting on me, I remained aware that a large sum of money could be involved, and at the same time the plan offered a sardonic mockery of the crowd, and of Pilate, too, for his belief in a crowd's sense of justice and compassion. I said suddenly, "All right. I'll drive the wagon, and keep track of you."

Since I knew my life now might be taking another turn, I communed with myself far into the night in my own room, quieting my nerves. At first it was hard to do, until I became aware that I might really be wanting some new turn in my life; so I got up and wrote a letter to my senator in Rome. I still have my copy of this letter. I told him I was tired of my life in Jerusalem, and asked if by this time all his business complications hadn't been cleared up, and the case settled. If this were so, I would rejoice in resuming my larger life with him in Rome. I missed him, I wrote. Would it be safe for him to use his influence and bring me hurrying back to Rome? And I told him that they were eating pasta here now, but it was never cooked properly. As he well knew, the pasta should be able to feel the bite.

Next day just before dark on my way to the Antonia stables to get a horse, I met Felix. This was another good omen, for after bantering with him I was able to tell him I was on my way to the little house of my girl, Mary of Samaria, and would not be back till morning, and we joked about my good luck in having such a girl. At the stables as I mounted my horse I told the same story to a groom, so it would appear I was off for the night, going where I had gone many times before. Then I rode to the city gate, passing through just as that blood-red sun vanished behind the hills, and soon I was in sight of the inn; and as I used to do when visiting my Mary, I went in for some wine, for the hours now would be long and slow.

Some travellers eating at the long table and talking in a language strange to me were the only guests. The grinning innkeeper assumed I was on one of my visits to the girl down the road. At other times he had remained aloof, but tonight, bringing the wine, he started talking and kept on, as if he had long ago placed me, and felt very comfortable in my presence. Having brought me a huge fat candle which lit up my corner and his own round face, he said, "Not long ago, just at sunset — down the road the other way from where you're going, by the olive grove — a man hanged himself."

"Who was it?" I said. "And what was the matter with him?"

"The man who came and cut him down said he had a paper on him. His name was Judas, Judas Iscariot. Isn't he the one they say betrayed the Galilean?"

"So they say," I said. It was all I could manage, I was so shaken. Shrugging, the innkeeper retired, and I picked up the jar of wine but couldn't drink. It seemed incredible that a young man so intelligent and well travelled could believe that a dead man was coming to meet him, a dead man he couldn't face. He was too ashamed, too disappointed in himself. And why? For telling the truth? At this moment, my hand trembled as I lifted the wine, and I knew for sure that he had told the truth. He preferred to kill himself rather than face the Galilean who was now as dead as a stone — this man he loved with a love that could turn to such shame, because he broke the silence and told the truth. What kind of self-respect was this? What kind of love? What kind of twisted pride? That he could believe the dead Galilean was coming his way and he couldn't face him was an offense against all nature. And I drank a lot of wine.

By the time I left the inn the stars were in their places in the clear sky I had seen so often over the Judean hills. Just ahead, back from the road a piece, was the little house that was mine — I had paid for it — with a light in the window. Checking my horse when I came to the house, I sat looking at the light, which meant she was in the house. Yet how could I tell whether she was alone? If followers of the Galilean were there with her, she could have nothing to say to me, nor I to her. And to see her now — would it be wise to see her on such a night, with Isaiah waiting? I remained there, a mounted man in the moonlight, staring at a small lighted window.

Finally I slapped the horse, and we trotted on for another mile. And then, stopping again, I looked back, finally turned back, remembering the news that many of the Galilean's followers had dispersed, giving up on him, which could mean that Mary herself, who used to have a lot of common sense, might now be disillusioned by his lack of any support, and might even be lonely and in need of the comfort I could give her. Yet back at the house again, I remained mounted, watching the window. The horse neighed, tossing his head, so I rode away before she came to the window.

At the designated turn some five miles along the road there was bright moonlight, yet I saw no one. Dismounting, I led the horse first one way, then another, till I heard a low whistle and Isaiah came out of the shadows. He led me into a little clearing hidden from the road by small trees, with a vineyard behind. A horse and wagon were in the clearing and two men; one of them was John and the other a huge bearded giant who seemed childlike and stupid. Isaiah and the other two had long curving swords in belted scabbards. I had my short Roman sword. Nothing as yet had been said.

Tying my horse to the back of the wagon, I saw a pile of blankets on the floor and one great blanket of leather strips sewn together. As I went to touch this leather, and drew back uneasily, I heard the others debating whether they should stretch out on the ground, or lie in the wagon. Since the dew was heavy on the ground they decided to use the blankets and the wagon, and soon I found myself half stretched out, huddling with them in the wagon. Some hours of waiting lay ahead, though Isaiah explained we would soon be moving back down the highway to a side road leading to the cemetery. Last night, watching at the cemetery, they had seen women guarding the tomb, staying there till the light changed in the sky. But there had been an interval when no one watched at the tomb. At the right time two or three strong men could quickly roll the stone away; only a few minutes would be required to carry the body down to the wagon where I would be waiting.

In the unearthly silence and with nothing more to be said, I hated myself for being there in the moonlit wagon with three men so alien I couldn't bear to make conversation. Then the huge childlike fellow startled me. He spoke; he said it was too bad the grapes on the vines weren't ripe, they were wonderful grapes — the best in the world. And having said this he curled up and went to sleep. We were too close together — I could smell their body odors, and I suffered. This land lacked water, these people needed water, Jerusalem always needed more water, and I thought of the beautiful baths of Rome and the sparkling fountains and got myself into a trance, while the big man snored and Isaiah and John stared with great intensity at the stars, even as Simon had done.

Some one star must have told Isaiah it was time to move, for he jumped out suddenly. We all hopped out and got the wagon on to the highway, my horse tethered behind it, and travelled back to the side road leading to the cemetery, moving slowly up this valley road to a place they had selected yesterday, back from the road and under a tree. Wasting no time, John went up the hill to the cemetery where he was to lie on the ground and watch the nearby tomb as he had done last night. In no time he returned, saying that three figures were near the tomb. We had to wait.

The hill at night had its own faint sounds, the sound of insects. The time passed slowly, the moon went behind some clouds. And these men remained silent; they could be silent for such a long time. Then John, who had been up the hill four times, returned to say that a man, joining the women, had taken them away with him, walking out of the cemetery, seeking some warmth, no doubt, since it had got so chilly. If they were gone for only a little while, there would be time enough for three of us to move the stone. Hopping out of the wagon, dragging out the great leather blanket, they went hurrying up the hill.

Standing by the wagon, I couldn't see them. It was pitch black; then the moon, breaking through clouds, put the whole hill in a shimmering glow, and I watched them move on the hill, then vanish. Only then did I look to the right at another hill, and knew what it was, and my recognition of it shook me. Trembling, I thought I could see the three silvered crosses against the dark sky, then something went wrong with my eyes or my mind and I couldn't see them. Coming to my senses, I realized that the crosses had been taken down. With the glow of moonlight gone, the hill without the crosses looked as if nothing had happened there that couldn't be soon forgotten; it had been a trick of the veil of light, the long, long light. Shivering, I tried to hear the tinkle of those little bells priests, women, and rich men wear on their coats to ward off demons. I knew nothing about the demonology of the tribes, except that they know demons are all around them. I was a stranger, I couldn't know what demons were trailing Isaiah and John. I felt so lonely, I got frightened. If I had had a little silver bell I would have tinkled it. I was in a place for bells, and for men who understood their power over evil.

Finally I heard sounds from the hill. First came the sound of small branches breaking, the fluttering, frightened chatter of some disturbed birds, then I could see them carrying the great rolled-up skin, carrying it carefully, the giant trailing them. Without even speaking to me, they put the body carefully in the wagon and jumped in. I did not get into the wagon. I couldn't. Not while I was thinking of Simon and the Galilean talking to each other. Untethering my horse, I mounted him just as their straining horse got the wagon out of ruts in the clearing and back on to the road. Following, I kept expecting to hear wild heartbroken cries coming from the hill.

When we had gone a short distance, the wagon stopped. Isaiah, giving the dull-witted sleepy giant a pat on the back and pointing to the hills, told him to go home. The giant disappeared into the darkness of the hills. Where their camp was, I didn't know, or want to know. I asked Isaiah where we were going. I didn't listen to what he said. In my mind I was riding hard, riding to the edge of the desert and some lonely barren crag in the wilderness. But when we went back along the highroad only as far as that clearing just off the road by the vineyard, I saw that Isaiah was right in going no farther. Already the stars, losing their brilliance, were receding.

On the other side of the highroad, just across from our clearing, was a hill littered with great and small rocks, all white in the moonlight, like patches of silver on a black wall. When the wagon was off the highway and safe in the clearing, they carried the great rolled-up blanket of skins across the road and up the hill to a site with three fairly large rocks. John had brought a shovel. They rolled these three stones from their resting place, not even asking me to help them, and quickly dug a shallow grave; then they rolled back the three stones which now marked the grave. Standing back, their hands on their hips, they sighed with great satisfaction, and we went back across the road to the wagon.

While I unhitched my horse, they were making beds with their blankets in the wagon, preparing to stay there the rest of the night, as they must have done on other night prowlings, since they seemed to know the clearing so well. We talked a little. Or rather Isaiah and I talked; John, who said not a word, had grown depressed. I didn't know what was the matter with him. Telling them I would return to this place by early afternoon, I rode slowly back to the city gate where the first dawnlight, touching the turrets, left the lower wall a black strip. Taking my time, I walked the horse till real sunlight fell on the walls, then I entered the city.

At the Antonia stable I encountered Marcellus, who

looked rested, fresh and happy, and he said in surprise, "Where have you been?"

"A girl," I said.

"An all-night girl, eh? Well, you certainly look it. Tell me something, Philo. I hear talk in the marketplace. What are the priests up to? What's going on? Is it true the Galilean said he would come back to life?"

"So I hear."

"Do his followers really believe he can do it?"

"So it seems. Why?"

"How far will they go backing him?"

"They stake everything on it, I think," I said, trying to get away.

"Have they any money?"

"Not your kind of money. They're poor people."

"They could all chip in, make up a purse. I'll give twenty to one he can't do it. Put the word out. Keep raising the odds till you see the greedy look come into their eyes. Oh, it'll come if they really believe it's a sure thing. And if a lot of them only chip in a little — go as high as fifty, a hundred to one. Look, you can hold the money. . . ."

"I want no part of it," I said testily.

"You need a good sleep, Philo," he called. "Get some sleep."

XXI

early as it was when I rode into the Antonia, the stable man was awake and able to tell me the prison captain had been so badly wounded in an ambush that he was now close to death. It had been a strange ambush, he said; just a flight of arrows from some bushes and no one there to pursue. This news did not make me grieve unduly. The captain now could tell no tales, and I took it as a good omen. At home I cleaned myself, got the smell of those farmers off me, and lay down.

Fortunately, I have trained myself to wake from sleep at whatever time I've told myself to. I don't know how I do this; I simply say to myself, I'm to be awake in two hours, or three hours, or six hours, and I find I'm awake. If I was to have my wits about me I needed three hours' sleep.

Three hours later I was up and out on the street, heading for the marketplace, then the temple's outer court. While I was still a great way off I saw people gathered in groups, and more coming. By the time I reached the great columns there was a real crowd, and mingling with them I listened. Some shouted, some argued fiercely, some made outraged protests. I got it all from little snatches of conversation I heard moving around. "Guards should have been placed at the tomb, Sanhedrin guards, never mind Pilate." "Why weren't they watched? Armed men could have kept those people away from the tomb." "Already they're saying he pushed the big stone away himself, and walked out as he said he would. People are flocking out there to see the empty tomb."

While I listened, I thought that the sound of my thumping heart could be heard by anyone brushing against me, and that some were already staring at me. I could hardly breathe. I had to get to the outskirts of the crowd. Even there I felt conspicuous till my friend Mordechai, the one with the lovely hands who played the harp at the physician's house, came from the inner court, dressed beautifully in some elaborate sacrificial costume. As he moved, little bells around his coat tinkled, a tinkling I had wanted to hear last night, and I called out to him, "Mordechai," and when he turned, I said, "Well, what you all feared would happen seems to have happened."

"And we're all fools," he said. "Fools who tried to behave correctly. Remember our silly talk about needing permission from Pilate? We talked and we talked, didn't we?" Dropping his voice, he said, "Philo, it's a hoax, but you know how stupid people are, and you know what they'll say, it's proof he's the Son of God. And they'll run around, saying it. I hear they're already coming out of hiding. I hear they're gathering on the Mount of Olives." Aware that two or three people were gathering around us, listening to him with great respect because of his position, he whispered, "These rumors, these absurd wild tales will grow, Philo. Something has to be done, something to show people it's a hoax, and done at any cost. I'm in favor of bringing all who might have had a hand in it before the Sanhedrin. Get it out of them, Philo. I'd beat it out of them." Pressing my arm, he began to make his way through the crowd, as I did too, and just beyond the columns a flock of little boys were being shepherded along by a bright-eyed thin young rabbi.

By this time, having all my wits about me, I had realized that fifteen or twenty people must have seen me in earnest conversation with Mordechai, which was good, very good, making it very easy, if he were to be the one I should approach later. I could say that someone seeing us talk had decided to use me, a stranger, someone obviously not involved. All the omens were good, the possibilities staggering. And making my way to the Mount of Olives, I wondered if Pilate, already on his way to Caesarea, was being told that the Galilean's followers, after smuggling his body out of the tomb, now claimed he had walked out himself. He would listen, I was sure, with some sardonic satisfaction.

Though the sun was directly overhead, its light was not harsh as was so often the case. The whole day ahead seemed likely to be in this warm happy light, and just ahead was the mountain slope with its tiers of streets, and sunlight brightening mountain greenery, and new warmth in shining rocks. On the lower slope, the streets with small stone houses had none of the luxury of the upper city, which was more familiar to me, though many of these houses also had pleasant gardens. If the Galilean really had had a following at all in Jerusalem it had been centered in this neighborhood; indeed, the house with the garden where he had dined the night he was seized and taken away was here, on the next street. Coming to this street I was astonished to see it filled with people. Little groups formed, split up, men and women — there were as many men as women — talking eagerly, then hurrying away from each other to join another group, eagerly seeking more information, the men looking baffled and anxious, the women with shining faces. Yet there was no clamor at all.

When a young man, little more than a boy, brushed by me, I grabbed his arm. "I've just come here," I said. "What's going on?"

"He came here," the boy said nervously.

"Who came here?"

"Jesus."

"Jesus!" and I must have had a strange expression on my face, for the boy drew away. Keeping a straight face, I said gently, "No, son, the Galilean is dead and buried."

"Not now," the boy said, his face a little wild. "He's the Son of God. He's done what he said he'd do. He's left the tomb. We've all seen the empty tomb," and pointing along the street where the crowd was getting bigger, he hurried away. Following him, I kept asking questions of people coming and going who were willing to talk, and they all took pride in having some bit of news I didn't have myself. The incredulity in my face seemed to delight them. After two or three of these quick conversations, I was able to put the story together. Mary Magdalene and another woman had gone to the tomb just after dawn. They had been there earlier. Now, returning, they found the great stone pushed aside and the tomb empty. Even though Mary Magdalene was the companion of Jesus and knew his great power, she was awed and fell down trembling. Then she and the other woman ran from the cemetery. They ran and stumbled and had to rest, and it took them a long time to get here and to the house down the street where her friends waited. After they had heard the amazing news, they all ran joyfully through the neighborhood shouting that the tomb was empty.

Then later, on this very street, and in the first early light, Mary Magdalene, having left the house, looked up suddenly and saw a young man approaching, though no one had been on the street when she started out. Coming closer, he called her, then called again, and she knew him, and when he was beside her, he did a thing only he could have done; smiling, he touched the lobe of her left ear, and at the intimate touch, she was suffused with warmth and joy. He talked to her. He told her to gather the disciples together so they could see and talk to him.

Well, it was her story. Imagine! And she wasn't a stupid peasant. Look what she was doing! How quickly she had realized the possibilities in the situation. And I was the one who had given her this golden opportunity to promote her dead magician.

I had come now to the house where so many people waited patiently. It was a stone house, a little larger than the others and with a garden; as I had been told, the disciples, having been summoned by Mary Magdalene, were in the garden conversing earnestly, looking like very ordinary men indeed, plainly dressed as they were, although I suppose I was seeing them through Judas's eyes. Some of them were excited, some threw their arms around exultantly, some looked subdued, half frightened now they had heard what they dared not hope to hear. They could believe because they had heard it from Mary Magdalene. One of them, stocky and half bald, started to weep, believing he would soon see his master, and I turned away uncomfortably.

I got well back from the crowd on the other side of the street. A little curly-haired boy kept throwing a ball to the roof of a two-story house, trying to judge where it would roll off the roof so he could catch it. As he missed the ball and it rolled to my feet, I tossed it to him, then saw Mary Magdalene coming along the street. Her face had never left me, and she had the walk of one of those high-waisted girls Simon had loved. I moved back toward the crowd and into her path so that she would be close in passing. Some were anxious to touch her, some backed away, half frightened. "Mary Magdalene," I said quietly, and she turned, and when her eyes remained on me I knew she remembered my face; for what other faces had she seen on that desolate hill when we had both watched the Galilean die and had both heard his last wild despairing cry and knew how dead he was now? Yet this! Here on this street. This!

Then suddenly I couldn't bear to get closer and question her. I was afraid if we talked she might really be questioning me, her eyes telling me she knew what I was up to; though surely now she was the one who should be questioned sharply. Her eyes were shining, and I knew they would go on shining no matter how cynical and scoffing my questions.

Bowing, and letting her pass by, I was deeply touched by the pathos of her radiance, for how easy it would be for her in her grief, loneliness, and mad love, which would have deepened as every hour passed, to start imagining things. When the mind is overwrought it is so easy to see phantoms, indeed, to see anything you want to see that may comfort you; and I realized with a pang that no matter how pathetic she might be in her delusions, she would dominate the others with the authority of her grace. The others, already ashamed of their own timidity, would willingly open themselves to her spell and soon come to believe they had seen and talked to the Galilean. The tomb was indeed empty. What good would it do if I went to her and said, "I know what happened at the tomb. I can show you. You're mistaken, Mary. Poor woman. You're carried away. . . . Don't go on doing this. . . ." But I was afraid of the change it might make in her. I was afraid of the sadness it might bring me.

It was easier to take sardonic satisfaction in my own role. There on the mountain was this wild fantasy and below at the temple were the scoffing angry Jews, who knew the fantasy might have serious consequences if they didn't quickly put an end to it. For once the disciples started telling how they had seen the Galilean, others would take it up, perhaps all across the city. And the empty tomb would always be there as a satisfying proof. And the disciples knew that they had had no hand in rolling back the stone.

Unless the Jews could find the body and display it with the marks of the crucifixion, and end the matter quickly, the Galilean's following could grow into a great multitude, crying out for the overthrow of the rich and the priests who had crucified the Son of God. Oh, that body! It was worth a king's ransom. I liked putting it this way. Since he had been executed as the King of the Jews, why shouldn't his people have the chance to ransom their king.

Walking home in lovely sunlight that made the real world beautiful, I had no qualms at all about the role I was playing. I only wanted to get some more sleep before riding out to Isaiah.

XXII

The king's ransom. Riding along the highroad, I kept asking myself how huge was a huge sum, and could there be any limit, if it was now a state affair, with no time for bargaining.

And here I have a point to make. A man's quick adjustment in his view of things seems to depend on how much money is involved. So I was already convinced I would be doing the tribes a great favor, and the deluded followers of the Galilean, too — as well as serving all natural things — by showing that death was inevitable for everyone. Riding by the house of Mary of Samaria, I hardly looked at it. I was certain she would have hurried to the Mount of Olives in her love of all marvellous things. The sun had set when I came to the turn in the road and that clearing, which I could see now was like a camping spot, with the vineyard near by. The wagon was there, the horse was grazing, and Isaiah and John, sitting cross-legged by a small fire, were taking food from a pot they had heated. As I dismounted, Isaiah threw away a bone, and John, standing up, wiped his mouth. They looked like two farmers, resting, eating, and feeding their horses before moving on. "Speak, man. Speak," Isaiah called sharply.

Taking my time and enjoying it, I tethered my horse to a sapling. Then, returning slowly, I told them about the mounting excitement in the city. I told them about the anger and disgust among Jews and about my talk with Mordechai, and finally, smiling broadly, I told them about the excitement on the Mount of Olives and the incredible stories of the Galilean having appeared on the streets, and how they were actually saying and getting people to believe that he had walked out of the tomb.

As I told of these things John began to stride up and down, circling around me nervously. The thing was getting too big for him. A naive man, he frowned a lot, trying to think. He worried about the stars. With night coming on, the first star had appeared in the sky. Out of the corner of my eye while I talked, I saw him stare intently at that one star, then look across the road at the side of that hill where the three stones marked the grave.

Isaiah, who had been listening quietly, pondering, suddenly jumped to his feet exultantly, dancing around the fire, jumping up and down. All the fine business prospects had not only dawned on him, they had suddenly been enormously magnified. "It's wonderful, it's grand, it's marvellous," he said. "Why bother with a man like Joseph of Arimathea when the higher priests, the whole Sanhedrin, will be dazzled by this?" Finally he sat down, off by himself, and pondered. Then he chuckled, waited, and chuckled again. "And they can't put us off. They'll want to see that body before it starts to rot."

I have often meditated on how men who secretly hate

each other can get together in a sympathetic under-standing and acceptance of each other when they have a mutual interest in getting a large sum of money. I have seen this happen in Rome and in Alexandria, and now it was happening here with me and Isaiah. It was my view that both Mordechai and Ezekiel should be approached. But everything had to be done quickly. "The body'll start to stink," he said. It was decided that I should get back to the city as soon as possible. In his turn, he said, he would see that the body was placed in the wagon and taken closer to the city; he had a friend who had a stable behind an abandoned little stone house near the wall. When this was done, I could tell my friends that the body was in a wagon near by — which he would keep an eye on from a distance. And since my friends trusted me completely, they could put the money in my hands, and when I had it, I could come to the stable, then return to them and confirm that the wagon was there, and then they could come to collect it, leaving us nothing to do but divide the ransom.

Then John, who had listened in morose silence, stood up, his hands on his hips. "It's not a good night," he said. "Not a good night. No." It was now dark, with just a circle of light from our fire. "We'll do it now," Isaiah said grimly. "It won't get any darker. The moon gets brighter." Giving John a thump on the shoulder to stir him, he led the way over to the wagon to get the shovel, leaving me squatting by the fire.

I felt the silence. I literally felt the weight of it in those moonlit Judean hills, something with a power of its own threatening me. I looked across the highroad at the slope of the hill, and as I watched I saw a figure crossing the road. Someone hiding in the little valley alongside the road had been watching us all the time. Jumping up, my hand on my sword, I went to cry out a warning to Isaiah and John. But my own horse neighed, a frightened animal cry. As I started to yell to Isaiah, the man came closer — and then for some reason I wasn't frightened, just mute with amazement.

In the moon's pale light I could tell that the man had a dark coat on. I couldn't see if the coat was brown, yet I was sure of it, and I thought the man was Judas, his death just a story; being quite insane, he had followed me here, keeping after me, just as he had come to my room. He came three steps closer, almost into the fire-light, and I heard one of those quick little interior whispers I can never recognize, but always trust: "It's not Judas." Then I choked; I couldn't cry out as he came closer and stood there as calmly as he had stood before Pilate in the judgment hall, his face friendly, waiting for me to speak.

Then Isaiah cried out, "What's that?" and as he came running towards us with his sword drawn, the man faded back to the highway, then along it and out of my sight. While I still trembled, Isaiah reached the road, looked all around, and then returned.

"You saw him?" I said, hardly able to get the words out.

"It was just a shadow," Isaiah said uneasily.

"We're being watched."

"It was just a shadow," he repeated. "There. See," and he pointed. "The tree. The wind blows the branches. Their shadows move in the moonlight. See," and convincing himself this was so, he laughed.

"The horse, the horse neighed."

"What's the matter with you? Are we scared of some shadows and a horse?"

And John said, "I heard the horse. What frightened the horse?"

"The same swaying shadows that frightened Philo. Come on, if we leave him there much longer he'll stink."

I stammered, "This is all wrong."

Isaiah was angry. "You want to leave him there?"

The nerves in my legs twitched so badly I had to sit down, and yet, though I was still trembling, I wasn't frightened. There had been no strange light; it hadn't been a vision that knocks a man down. We had seen a real man, which was why I was stunned, but not frightened. Looking around, making sure where I was, and staring at the sky to see if it was the same, I said, "He's not there."

"What?" he said, startled. "Not in his grave now?"

"No."

"Are you mad, Philo?" But something in my manner worried him. "Come on," he said. "We're going to take a look at that grave," and he started up the embankment.

"No," I yelled. "He's not there," and I caught his arm.

Amazed, he stared at me. "You know he's not there?" Then, full of sudden distrust of me, he shouted, "All right, we're going to look at that grave right now. Come on."

"It's no use. He's not there."

He grabbed at my shoulder, shouting. "What have you been up to? Where is he?" And now his big hands were on my throat. Trying to tear his hands away as he swung me around, backing me over the fire, I gasped, "I don't know." His grip tightened on my throat. He was far too big, too heavy. My eye sockets were burning with pain, blackness closed in on me as his scarred face came against mine. "Tell me. Where is he?" I dropped my hands. I drew my short sword, and as he literally lifted me up by the neck I drove the sword deep in him, and suddenly free, I staggered, trying not to fall, kicking up the fire. Then I saw him lurching, his face bobbing into the firelight, his hands on the blade. Then he fell near John, who, bewildered and moonstruck, hadn't moved. I knew Isaiah was dead, and John knew it too.

Moving as if coming out of a trance, John circled slowly around Isaiah's body, ignoring me, then, halting, looked up raptly at his one star. Suddenly he uttered one long, wild shriek. Rushing at the horse, John untethered it, got blankets from the wagon, rolling them rapidly and throwing them like a saddle across the horse's back, and then there was only the sound of hooves as the old wagon-horse raced away, racing on as he would till he dropped. From far along the road came one more crazy lonely cry — as if John had seen demons riding with him — and I knew he would head blindly for the desert, the wilderness of his fathers.

I looked down on Isaiah, his leg on a smouldering ember, and thought of Simon. Isaiah had grown a beard, just like Simon's, but the head still didn't look at all like Simon's. I wiped my blade on Isaiah's shoulder. Then I realized I should get out of there as quickly as possible, but as I mounted my horse, I saw the shovel near the fire. It shouldn't be left there, or anywhere near by. Dismounting, I picked it up and rode with it well along the road, well away from the slope of that hill, threw it into the bushes, then rode, riding hard, my mind in such a whirl I could hardly see the road, as I tried to ask myself the right questions.

Had I really seen the Galilean, or was I overwrought? No, Isaiah had also seen him. Isaiah had chased after him with his sword. What better witness than a murderous thief? So the man had really been there. But why me? Why did the Galilean show himself to me? Was it because of Judas talking so much to me? And now Judas became part of my whole amazement. How had Judas known for sure that the Galilean would appear, how had he known it with so much more certainty than any of them, even Mary Magdalene? Yes, she had really seen him and talked to him. I knew now it was as she said.

The horse was tiring from the hard riding as I kept asking myself, Why me? Why me? I don't know the answer. I'll never know.

Near the city I turned and looked back at the moonlit hills. No one would know where that grave was, no one should ever know, or break the silence. And this gave me a satisfaction I couldn't fathom, so I looked up at the stars, aware that I had had a hand in an event that could have magnificent importance.

XXIII

Since all my nervous energy and excitement had turned so quickly into fighting for my life with Isaiah, the shock I got from seeing the Galilean had been delayed: delayed, too, by my over-stimulated imagination on the wild ride home. Not till I had flung myself on the bed did I really begin to feel the shock, and soon I was in bad shape. Little nervous tremors ran through me. My whole sense of reality kept slipping away until I was afraid to sleep. All next day I was troubled and uneasy about where I was, whether I was in my room, or out on the street. It took two days for me to come to my senses. Even then I had to control my impulse to hurry back to the highroad and look at the slope of that hill and see if the three stones had been moved. I knew if I did this it would be an insult to my own intelligence, and anyway, under no circumstances could I afford to be seen near that wagon and Isaiah's body. It would be madness.

It was unthinkable, and yet I kept on thinking about it. Soon I was telling myself I could ride out there and be back in one hour, and no matter what was in store, I had better do it, or I would have no rest, no real peace of mind, for the rest of my days. So I had to do it. In the middle of the afternoon with the sun bright and the air clear, I screwed up my courage, went to the stables, and rode out. I rode past the inn, and on past Mary of Samaria's house, not even looking in that direction. And when I came to the turn and that clearing which was back from the road, I did not turn in to see if the wagon was still there. No one was on the road. Without dismounting, I rode slowly along the embankment on the other side of the road while I scanned the slope of the hill. The sun shone through trees on the rocks, but as I moved along slowly one tree then another blocked my view. I couldn't see the stones. I thought they had been moved. I was in a panic. Then, there it was! I could see the three stones, all in place. All untouched. Slapping the horse, I got back on the road, trembling with relief. I don't know why — because I still wasn't sure what had happened to me.

His grave was there, undisturbed, though I had seen him here last night, looking at me and friendly, and it couldn't have been just a vision, for Isaiah had seen him, too. So, something more than a vision. I'm not saying he was flesh and bone, a body coming out of the grave. Yet he was real. Just as real as the horse under me. Yet not of this flesh. So something of another substance that as yet we do not know — just as the mind's power is a force we do not understand. And so it was most likely as Simon had said: Death would be a big brother looking after him, a part of the grandeur of life. The Galilean had shown me that death was not an enemy, just a change in the rhythm of life. But why me? Why me? And it didn't matter where the Galilean's bones were. They weren't needed in his new bright enlargement. While my wonder grew, I had a sense of reality widening as I looked all around, with everything — trees, rocks, the horse, the nearby vineyard, even the sky — coming so close that they hurt and brought tears to my eyes. As Judas had said in his story, I now saw that the Galilean in his magic substance could be all around me, even under the horse's hooves, or in the wing of the bird swooping from a tree toward the sun. I galloped away, got home within the hour, and began to look around at what was happening.

My physician, who evidently saw no change in me, told me that guards from the Sanhedrin had seized known followers of the Galilean, taking them one by one, and questioning them roughly and ruthlessly, even the women, trying to find out where the body had been taken. They even questioned Joseph of Arimathea, but saw that he, on his own, was baffled and deeply troubled. They respected Joseph. He was a rich man.

When I heard these stories and remembered the joy I had seen on faces of the Galilean's followers on the Mount of Olives, telling of his appearance, I wondered why crowds hadn't gathered at the temple. Why hadn't peasants flocked in from the countryside? Why hadn't the poor in the lower city done as I had heard those Canaanites say they would do — come rushing to the temple crying, "Truly he is the Son of God. See him now. He is our king." The Sanhedrin, I was sure, were prepared for these demonstrations, and maybe the Romans were too, although Pilate had not returned from Caesarea.

Why did I not go to the Mount of Olives and seek out Mary Magdalene? Well, I couldn't bear to face this one person who might share all my wonder. But she had her story, and I felt that no one should ever try and change it, and besides, with that lovely woman I would have had to drop my mask and tell the truth. But her truth, even my truth now, was doing all right as it was; the way things were working out began to appeal to my heart and my imagination. The truth, it seemed to me, was that no demonstrations had taken place because the followers of the Galilean, supposed to be a multitude, hoped to see him appear in the flesh. If they could have seen him walk out of the tomb, they would have cheered. They would have cheered even louder if they had seen him coming into Jerusalem at the head of a parade and shouted, "He is our king." Flesh and bone. In their longing for the truly marvellous they had to see and touch the flesh themselves. Trying to believe that Mary Magdalene had seen and talked to him, as had some of the others, it was said that they asked dubiously, "Yes, but where is he?"

The news was that the crowd on the Mount of Olives, who had been close to him, were out in the open, organizing with great fervor, though small in numbers. Their new energy and happiness about things as they were now gave me some cynical satisfaction. They obviously were the only ones who had the truth, they said, so they should have control of it too; and since they were very peaceful, depending for their strength only on their faith, the Jews who still scoffed at the story about the tomb and a resurrection began to view them as harmless and even permitted them to meet in the synagogues.

I had learned from Judas about a man's terrible compulsion to tell the truth and how this truth may break a thousand hearts, and his own, too, so I talked to no one about the Galilean. I did not even permit myself to see

Mary of Samaria; if I drank with her and felt all her sensual appeal, the drink and my desire would loosen my tongue and get me talking. Even with my Ezekiel, who was always so frank with me, I found myself holding back, hardly drinking at all. And I never talked about the Galilean, which was difficult for me since there now were many stories about him appearing somewhere in the countryside and doing something marvellous. But no one among the Jews or Romans took these stories seriously.

I kept track of these things, though my mind was on Rome now. Every night I dreamed of Rome. I had a hunch I was to hear soon from the senator. I had even told Marcellus I was to hear from him. When letters came from Rome and I didn't hear, Marcellus' smiling eyes used to hurt me.

I was with Marcellus the day our postmaster handed me my letter. Marcellus watched my trembling hand. Yes, the letter was from the senator; it was not a long letter, and deliberately made to sound like a business note, I was sure. The senator said he was most anxious to have me back in Rome working with him again and he was sure my former associates would express their regret that I had ever left Rome. I knew this meant that all charges had been dropped; the outraged citizens had all been mollified, pacified, and in their purses satisfied. Giving Marcellus that same pitying smile I had so often got from him, I said, "I'm to return to Rome as soon as possible. The senator is anxious to see me." It was so hard for me to believe what I was saying, I started to laugh. "So, I was wrong," Marcellus said quietly. "Yes, I thought he would let you rot here. Why not? It was expedient." On Marcellus' right cheek there was a healing scar from a bandit's arrow that had grazed the cheek. The scar looked grotesque on his delicate handsome face. "Back in Rome — good for you," he said, gripping my right hand, his left hand on my shoulder. Though he smiled warmly, all his own longing for Rome was in his eyes, and the pain, too, of knowing for sure that his family would manage to keep him away. "Let's drink, Philo."

Taking my arm, he marched me all the way to our tavern, where we drank. Soon he was a little drunk. He kept saluting my astonishing faith in the senator till he finally fell silent, brooding for a long time. Then suddenly appearing to brighten, he said he had written a long poem in the style of Propertius, even using Propertius' golden Cynthia. Now he would recite as much of the poem as he could for me. Around us in the dimly lit tavern were the tough faces of Roman soldiers, and these faces came leaning closer because Marcellus did not keep his voice down.

I tried to listen, but my thoughts were all of the senator as I tried to cope with the wonder of his loyalty to me. That such a corrupt, ruthless man, such a master of chicanery, should have been unwilling to betray my faith in him grew more and more astonishing. He didn't need me. He could easily do without me, and yet he had kept faith with me, and as my wonder grew I thought of Simon. He, too, hadn't betrayed me. In the eyes of all good respectable men, Simon was disreputable, murderous, ruthless, and wherever he was, always an outlaw, yet he couldn't turn informer, not even to bargain for his life. The informer! Was it the ultimate secret degradation? I could never have brought myself to inform on the senator. Off by myself now, I tried to understand the nature of these two men, who themselves did not care for good reputations, yet found a betrayal of faith intolerable. Why? What was it in them? As I sat back, moved and pondering, there must have been tears in my eyes, for Marcellus, who had gone on reciting, paused, looking proud and happy, believing that his poem was moving me deeply.

XXIV

There were things going on in the back of my mind now that I did not quite understand or try to deal with until the day after drinking with Marcellus when I encountered Joseph of Arimathea coming from the temple. I asked him in an offhand manner, as if it were just an idle thought, if he had heard what had happened to that woman, Mary Magdalene. Stroking his beard — I never knew what went on in that man's mind — Joseph said she was not playing any role in organizing the Christian community, though she was still living in it — they were calling themselves Christians now. And then, shrugging, he said, "I don't think they want her around now. She was the one who was really close to the Galilean, and, besides, there's that story going around that she used to be a fallen woman. You can understand they don't want to hear from her, eh?" And then his tone became sarcastic. "They let her do a woman's things. Prepare meals and so on, hoping, I suppose, that she keeps what she knows to herself." And he laughed and left me.

My common sense told me that my mind should be on Rome now and not on local matters. This is a mistake, a real mistake, I said to myself as I made my way up the hill to the neighborhood and the street where I had last encountered the woman. Today on this street everything looked very peaceful, with children playing in the sunlight, and I asked a curly-haired boy with huge brown eyes if he knew where Mary Magdalene lived. Moving out to the middle of the dusty road, he pointed to a little stone house far along the street. The wind blew dust in my eyes as I tried to make out the house. I had no plan. Yet it seemed important that there should be nothing in my mind till I was with her. When I knocked on the door no one answered.

Walking around the house, I sat down in a neat little garden. It was so carefully tended one could have believed she had a gardener who skillfully arranged these flowers in a whole gaiety of patterns. Sitting there I daydreamed, pretending that she had a servant, and the servant now was saying, "There is someone, a man, a young man, waiting in the garden." But finally I went back to the dusty road, walking away, but never too far. Carts passed me, and a very stout woman waddling along with three children, and then three workmen, carpenters carrying some lumber and a short ladder.

Then, more than a hundred feet away from the house, I turned and saw her coming along the street. I knew her by her light and easy unsubmissive walk, flowing along toward me in a light blue robe gathered at the waist by a wide rose-colored band, the two thick tassels hanging on her hips, and I let her go into the house. Then, after giving her a little time to get settled — while telling myself I must be careful not to mention Judas, since his story could only shock and hurt her — I went to her door. And when I knocked, there she was, leaning out a little, her face only a foot from mine, her eyes on me, her eyes like the sunlit blue sea a little too far apart, her mouth a little too big, her nose too, but this irregularity, which broke all the rules of beauty to give an immense and unexpected pleasure, made me feel shy.

"I think you know me," I said finally.

"Yes. I remember you . . . that day . . ."

"We spoke. Remember?"

"You looked so alone."

"So did you. My name is Philo of Crete."

"Philo. Well, what is it, Philo?"

"I'm a scribe," I stammered, trying to smile. "There are things that ought to be written down. I should talk to you. It seems to me that so much that has happened here comes back to you. Forgive me, but in my imagination I have talked and walked with you. Can I come in?"

Nothing was said while she eyed me boldly, then suddenly something in her steady glance gave me a little lift. "Come in, Philo," she said, and then in the small white room she was motioning me to a chair. And while she herself went to the low silken couch I stood looking around, baffled by the sense of elegance I got from the room that had only the plain white walls, a Persian rug, the two chairs, the couch, and some short and tall colored jars, wondering if this suggestion of elegance came from the colored jars or from the way they were arranged to make all other decorating unnecessary. Or could it come from the garden light from the window almost down to the floor, the sunlit flowers in all their gaiety behind the window. She was smoothing back her long black hair.

"It's very dusty on the road," she said, "I should have

worn a shawl. You say you are a scribe for the Romans?"

"Yes, but I am returning to Rome."

"But you are not a Roman?"

"A Greek from Crete. Tell me, Mary, was the Galilean ever in Crete?"

"Why do you ask?"

"In Crete there are some ancient paintings from the ruins of Thera. I loved those paintings. I'm sure the Galilean would have loved them too. Some day I would like to show them to you — some day . . ."

"You're here to tell me this?" she asked, smiling.

"I'm sorry. As I say, I'm a scribe. Well, your friends are all telling their stories. I hear these stories. The thing is, Mary, why is there nothing about you, nothing about the way it was between you and the Galilean, in any of these stories? Why is this, Mary? I thought you might want me to be your scribe and tell your story."

"My story?" she asked softly, wonder in her eyes.

"Yes."

"What moves you to do this, Philo?"

"I don't know."

"This is strange, very strange," she said with a faint smile. "No one else around here comes to me."

"The truth is," I began, fumbling the words. "The first time I saw you — well, I seemed to know you."

"On that day?"

"On that day."

"Well," she began, and seemed to be off by herself, and far away from me. Then she said, "Why?"

"I know you can't stay here."

"How do you know?"

"Your friends are saying you're not much needed. No. Worse. You are even pushed aside." Having spoken so brutally, I waited while two spots of color appeared on her cheeks, then I said, "I know this is presumptuous of me, but I feel we have been together in something. Don't ask me what," I said, dreading what I might blurt out under her eyes. "Even though you do not know what we have shared," I stammered, growing more confused as she looked at me with such curiosity.

Something I said must have touched her imagination; for, getting up, she took a jar of wine from a lovely cypress casket and two small bowls and filled them with wine, and gave one to me. Then, just eyeing each other while not a word was spoken, we drank the wine. When we put down the bowls she took my hand with a little laugh that inspired in me a most extraordinary sense of intimacy and said, "Thank you for coming, Philo. I think I was waiting to talk to someone."

The sense of warming ease I felt in her did not last long. Her mood changing, she stood up, moving to the window, where she stood looking out. In the long silence I felt saddened and diminished. "Yes, it's a lovely little garden," I said finally.

"Yes, I like it," she said, not turning.

"I sat out there waiting for you," I said. "I was day-dreaming in the garden. I seemed to see you coming to me there...."

"And just think," she said, "they let me have this little house all to myself."

"All by yourself."

Finally she turned. Although her blue robe hid her body, as she came toward me there was an easy rippling rhythmic effect in her movements that made me think only of her body. Again taking my hand and with friendly amusement in her eyes, she said, "Sit down here beside me, Philo, my scribe, and tell me something about yourself and what brought you here." I talked to her about Crete, about Rome, and the good rich life I was to have in Rome, and I only made her restless. She got up, walking the length of the room, pausing sometimes, lost in thought.

"I like you, Philo," she said gently.

And I said, "Then I'm happy."

She said, "I think I'd trust you, yes, Philo," and her hand came out to my arm. "Yes, it's lonely for me here now, Philo," she said. Then frowning, she went on, "Yes, it's lonely. Good men, staunch men, have everything in their hands." The mist in her eyes and her parting lips held me so rapt I heard my heart beating. "He needed them, but not as he needed me." I could not place the faint accent or the modulations of her low voice, and I could not tell where she came from as I watched her get up, restless again and moving around. Coming back toward me now, she passed so close that the heavy rose tassels tied on her hip brushed against my head, and as she turned again, the blue robe swung away from her bare ankle. And though she hadn't even glanced at me, I felt first a little catch in my throat, then such a jolt at all my sensual longings that I knew for sure what it was about her that prompted men in the countryside, and women, too, to decide with satisfaction that she, not Mary of Samaria, was the one who had been the whore before she took up with her Galilean lover. She was the woman all men wanted when near her; all men were willing to believe she could have a hundred lovers, yet offer each one of them serenity and ecstasy.

"Mary, Mary," I whispered, going to her and taking both her hands. "You know the stories," I said. "I know you never were a whore."

"How do you know?" she asked calmly.

"I just know."

"I see."

"Didn't it hurt you to hear these things when you were out in the countryside?"

"When I was with him? Oh, no," she said and at the sound of her sudden warm laughter I felt my skin tingle and I wanted her; and in my need and my stiffening, my face burned. Holding onto myself I felt a sexual shiver almost like a pain; and trying to turn from her I wondered if this strange lifting swirl of the imagination came from knowing who she was and where she had been, or whether any man in another country might be so touched by her.

"You see, Mary," I began, "around here among your friends — they must know how much the Galilean needed you."

"I'm sure they know," she said, "and it's true he needed me. Yes, Philo, you've guessed it. If you're needed, much that is said out loud seems foolish to you, and my friends only know what he said out loud," and she nodded, smiling to herself. "The other things," she went on, "the other things, the secret things, the night things, the whispered things, or the silent things — I know this side of him."

"And your friends know you do, eh?"

"I think so."

"I can see why they wouldn't want you around."

"No one has asked me to leave."

"But you will leave, won't you?"

"I think so."

"Where will you go? Look Mary," I said, my heart beating heavily. "Have you thought of Rome? I have friends there who will help you."

"No. I'm going into Egypt."

"Egypt," I said, my face burning. "Well, wherever you go men will look at you and want you."

"Then it will be up to me to be what I am," she said, rising and leading me to the door, where, taking her hand impulsively, I kissed it, and blurted out, "You saw him, they say. Have you seen him again? Where is he?"

"Where there's love."

"I'd have to know something more."

"It's all you need to know."

"Then goodbye, Mary," and I started down the road. When I looked back she was still standing at the door, watching me as if she knew her secrets could have been going with me, but weren't and never would. And even when I turned again, she was still watching with a faint smile I've never been able to fathom.

XXV

The day I left Jerusalem I knew I was leaving it forever. If the city had had a song for me, it now had another song which I did not want to hear till I was far, far away, though I knew I would surely hear it no matter how far away I was. On the day of my return to Rome I found that city all in sunlight, not the harsh Judean sunlight, but softer and more comforting, and over the whole city lay that bluish Roman light from the blue sky above as if Aphrodite herself had thrown her light blue mantle protectively over the whole city. On that first day I knew what it was about Rome that I liked so much; it was its openness; a city open to the whole world, not walled in at all. In the whole countryside no town was walled in. Even the temples were open to the sky, the wind, and the people.

The senator's handsome villa in Tibur had been the house of his father, a very successful general with the legions in Germany, who had lost his money in bad speculations, which was why the senator, his son, could never believe he had enough money. I got there late in the afternoon. Tired and dust-covered, I found him waiting to greet me. "Philo, my dear Philo," he cried, throwing his arms around me. He looked older, heavier, almost bald now; the skin at his neck was looser, too, and he had found an extra chin, but he had the advantage of really looking like a senator. He had the square face, the noble head, the shrewd eyes, and weight in his manner; a man who could afford to be at ease with everyone. He had also the splendid patrician manner and a cultivated voice. These rich men who have established themselves and have the right connections exude a sense of well-being I have always found attractive. "We won't talk now, Philo," he said, "but man, how we'll talk while we eat! We'll have a feast, Philo. Bathe now, rest and dress. It's time to get the dust of the provinces out of your blood."

A servant took me to my room, where new clothes were laid out for me and a bath prepared, and when I had bathed and examined my new fine clothes, smiling to myself all the while, I lay down. Then as soon as I closed my eyes I thought of Livia, my young dead wife, the senator's daughter! I heard her laughter, I saw us in the places where we had made love secretly in this villa, a long time ago, a long long time ago. I fell into a heavy sleep. And hours later when my servant woke me, I sat up mumbling a Judean name, startling the servant. I didn't know where I was. I got dressed and joined the senator for our little feast.

Though there was just the two of us, he had brought in three dancing girls in the roles of the muses, and musicians too. With these three pretty girls gathered around him trying to banter with him and tease him, he lay back on a couch lost in thought. One of the girls, little and pert and black-eyed and looking like an imp, caught my eye. Rising, the senator took my arm, leading me to the table. He had taken off his sandals, and walking in step with him, I looked at his big square-toed feet as they came down so firmly, and remembered how I had thought of them that night in the Judean hills when Simon had questioned me. A man has to believe in something, and oh, how hard I had tried to believe in those determined feet.

While I ate and drank and watched the dancing girls, the senator, a real glutton himself, told me about his long campaign to silence those merchants who had brought the charges against him. It had been a long and a costly campaign. There had been many postponements, some severe beatings, and one or two deaths before the charges had been dropped and everybody was satisfied. "These things, you see, take time, Philo," he said, shrugging. "The more upright the accuser, the longer it takes and the costlier it is."

"You know the ways of Rome, I'm sure of that," I said.

"I always measured the size of the bribe by the weight of the merchant's outrage. More outrage, more money," he said.

"Money. Yes, it always gets down to money," I said.

"Morality is expensive," he said, smiling. "A virtuous upright man costs three times as much as an ordinary cheating merchant. Let everybody know, Philo, that you are a virtuous upright man. There's money in it."

As he chuckled I felt the warmth of his goodwill to me and also his own vast satisfaction that he had been able to walk roughshod over the law courts, the qualms of other business men, and the public conscience, and at the same time leave everyone as satisfied as he was himself.

"You are a magician," I said.

"Rome is full of my kind of magician," he said cynically. "Well, tell me about Judea, Philo. Were things so quiet? Just peace and good order?"

"Well, there were no great riots while I was there. There was a Galilean who was executed."

"What for?"

"Blasphemy. Did you hear about it here?"

"Why should we? Blasphemy. A common thing, I suppose, among those people," and then he smiled. "Well, this time you kept out of trouble."

"I was a scribe."

"And not involved. I understand. Just the same, you are an impulsive man, Philo, and you seem to like those Jewish women. Anyway, here we are, Philo," and his pleasure at having me there was so apparent I was profoundly moved. It would have been so easy, so much less trouble, so much more expedient, for him to have dumped me, so why hadn't he? I wondered, watching his puffed and flushed face as he went on with his eating. Were there some things he could not do? What was it that wouldn't let him do these things? I watched him and wondered while he talked about Pilate's political prospects after the inevitable return from Judea.

"Just a minute," I said suddenly. "Tell me something. Why did you keep on with it? It would have been so much easier to have betrayed my faith in you."

"Why?" he repeated, looking surprised. Then, after reflecting, and smiling to himself, he said, "In every man there must be a secret domain. It's a mysterious thing, isn't it?"

Sighing and closing his eyes, the senator finally said, "Enough about Pilate tonight. Ah, you're young, Philo. You're still fresh. But I must rest." Exhausted by the wine and food he might be, but as he got up he beckoned to one of the muses and took her to his bed. After daydreaming for a while, I too went to bed, taking with me that pert and impish little black-eyed girl who was a delight with her soft laughter and sense of mischief, even in bed.

In the middle of the night I woke up. Suddenly wide awake, I listened in the dark as if trying to hear voices that might have been talking to me while I slept. Soon I began to feel exhilarated, and in the dark I was smiling to myself, for it seemed right, yet wonderful and so true to life, that I had got from so cynical, worldly, and corrupt a man as the senator an insight into the Galilean.

XXVI

My life in Rome now took an opulent commercial turn and I was very busy. Though I lived up at the villa and always would spend weekends there, they were preparing a place for me on the other side of the Tiber where I could entertain merchants from cities throughout the empire. I had a young slave and a litter. The senator, in high favor again, had decided it would not be expedient for me to return to Alexandria and handle the wheat sales again, so I became his lieutenant here in Rome. We were involved in tin mining, lumbering, wheat, oil, imported wines, anything that could show a profit on a large scale, and the mixture of scholarship and business shrewdness I displayed in handling the foreign merchants delighted the senator. I got to know the Roman women again. I got to know all the politicians, too, was at home with the more patrician families, and for two years did not really try to cope with what had happened to me in Judea, though when I looked at the sea, or stood by a river I thought of the Judas story I had preserved so carefully.

Then, on idle weekends when I was up at the villa I began to work away at the whole story. It was as if I knew I had to finish it. And I did finish it.

But just when I was ready to put it out, I met Pilate at a big gathering at the senator's villa. Recalled after his savage slaughter of the Samaritans, he hadn't been given another post, nor would he get one, they said. But he had been well looked after; a friend, close to the emperor, had had him put money in the mines in barbaric Cornwall, and in no time he had become very rich.

Now, with his wife beside him, jesting with a tall hard-faced general just back from Gaul, his eyes kept shifting around restlessly. Until he turned to his wife, I thought he looked like another one of those very successful disappointed men. But as he and his wife exchanged intimate little smiles, their ease and warmth with each other astonished me. The last time I had seen them together in Judea she'd had the eyes of a woman who knew her husband had betrayed everything in himself that she held most dear. Yet now as she stood beside him, her hand reached out for his, her fingers twining, then untwining, and twining again around his, and no one could have believed that she had once despised him. I could not take my eyes off her still-lovely face, wondering how they had recovered their sacred private domain, even as I touched his arm.

Startled, turning with his old commanding apartness, he recognized me, then laughed. Taking my arm, moving me away from his wife and the general, he said, "Philo! Well, Philo. And I've heard you've done very well here." I agreed I had been lucky after the senator had got me out of Judea. As we talked amiably about Judea, I was fascinated to see that he had lost his bitterness and had no bad memories of the province or the Jews. "I'll remember them as a stubborn and difficult people," he said. "They have a world of their own. I could never feel at home in that world," and he smiled. "But who would want to be, Philo?"

Among all the Romans in Jerusalem, Pilate and his wife were the only ones whose lives had been shaken by the Galilean. And moved that I was here with them now, I said, "The Galilean. Remember the Galilean?"

"The Galilean," he repeated, and as he reflected, frowning, I thought he was going to say he didn't remember him. "Yes. His brown coat. I remember. I liked him."

"You were right in feeling the way you did about him."

"Was I? Well, it was a ritual killing," he said, shrugging. "I made it clear I would have no part of it. Do you remember, Philo? I, as a man, could have no part in it. It was just my office that was used for their sacrifice. The man in my office could not intervene."

"Yet the Galilean was no ordinary man, was he?"

"Yes. There was something in him — whatever it was —" and he turned to glance at his wife, who was talking with great animation with the general. "My wife saw something in him, even more than I did," and again he looked at her fondly. "Something a woman loves. She's a Roman. Roman women fall in love easily with exotic figures in foreign lands." Though he kept his little affectionate smile, he was now wondering, bemused, even happily enchanted by what had happened for him with his wife. "She thought I should intervene," he said, half to himself, "and she had contempt for me. It lasted a long time. There was pain, Philo. A lot of pain, and then," and with wonder in his blue eyes again, he said, "she came to see that I had no choice. How did she come to see it?" and he shook his head. "I think it was the story about the empty tomb. The story getting bigger all the time, and she heard it. It dazzled her. The shock, the wonder of that empty tomb, and you know, Philo, she saw then that I couldn't intervene." And he smiled. "There's nothing like an empty tomb."

"I know about that empty tomb," I whispered, looking around and feeling I was suffocating.

"Who doesn't know about it now," he said smiling.

"I know why it was empty," I whispered nervously, frightened by the blind and reckless urge in me to keep on talking after holding back for so long. But there flashed in my mind, oh, so vividly in my mind, that figure on the roadside in the moonlight, the man in the brown coat, moving closer to me, allaying the fright in me; and as soon as I started to talk I felt relief, even though Pilate's blue eyes never left my face as he leaned closer so that he could hear every word.

I had enough control of myself to conceal my relationship with Simon, and that I was in on the thing from the beginning. Let Pilate divine it if he wanted to. But I told him how the two bandits, knowing of my good connections, had come to me to act as a go-between arranging the ransom for the body, and how I had met them at night so they could show me where they had buried the body in the shallow grave on the hillside, and how, when they were ready to take the body and put in in their wagon, I had seen the Galilean. "It was more than an apparition," I whispered fervently. "Then I couldn't go near that grave. I fought with Isaiah. I killed him. I rode away, wildly."

"A ghost," he said, shaken, his eyes far away from me.

"It wasn't a ghost," I whispered. "I had the best witness in the world. A thug who doesn't care about such things. Isaiah. He ran to the road after him. The grave is still there."

"Still there," he repeated uneasily, turning slowly toward his wife, who, this time, met his eye, and as she smiled, her hand went out to him, the fingers beckoning. All her peace of mind, her regained love and respect, was in her smile and beckoning hand, and I saw behind her those two birds circling slowly over that bare hill. I saw this just as Pilate, turning to me, pale and shaken, said, "Oh, you reckless, interfering fool."

"Sir . . ." I began, shaken myself.

"Why do you tell this story now?"

"I'm only telling it to you."

"Why tell it to me now?"

"It's the truth."

"Who says it's the truth?" he said, clutching my arm angrily. His fingers hurt me. I tried to pull away. Then he changed, the change in him filling me with dread, for he was as cold and quiet and sure of himself as he had ever been when I had known him as the Procurator of Judea.

"The gods don't like a man who violates sacred places, bringing disorder and unhappiness," he said. "Here in Rome, Philo, you are a criminal who desecrated a tomb. It could be hard on you," and his smile frightened me. "Who else knows about this?"

"No one else on earth. I swear."

"Bury it, Philo. Bury it so deep in your heart no one can ever dig it out. If one word of this should ever get to my wife and upset her, I'll know that word must have come by way of you, and I'll have you killed, Philo," and turning his back on me abruptly, he joined his wife. And I knew I must never again be in the presence of Pilate and his wife, and I knew, too, that I should avoid those Christian bands that had begun to appear in Rome.

These Christians seemed to take it as a sign of merit that nobody liked them, and certainly they didn't appeal to me. Yet, in spite of my common sense they had a fascination for me. On corners or in marketplaces, I listened to them tell their wild stories about what had happened in Judea, while they sat around waiting happily for the end of the world, and I heard them tell how a rat of a man named Judas had betrayed the Galilean out of a greed for money. The loathsome man. The sinister evil bloodsucker.

And it troubled me, knowing as I did that they were only saying all the things Judas knew they should say; it was as if they were only playing their part, as he had played his. Was he to be the scapegoat forever? Was that it? I wondered. But what could I do? Pilate would have me killed if my story came out. So, it was for me here in Rome now as it had been in Judea; I had to be silent. I didn't like it at all. I couldn't bury the story in my heart and forget it, as Pilate had suggested. I had it written down. It existed now.

Sometimes I took out the manuscript, looked at it, and told myself bitterly that it had more wonder and mystery than the story they had accepted. The only thing that fascinated me was that Judas, in their story, was where the Galilean had asked him to be. No one knew he was really the loving servant, serving faithfully in the terrible role he had accepted. It was as if the secret had been kept, as if he had never talked too much. The Galilean was having his way. And Pilate with his threat was insisting that the Galilean should go on having his way. But they couldn't take the story from me. I waited. And I was afraid to talk about it even to my Julia, the girl who lived with me, looking after me when I got sick or had the pains in my legs.

The night Pilate died — it was an early death, not from battle wounds, but from a kind of malaria that he had picked up in Judea and that had kept recurring year after year — I was moved and deeply troubled. I had admired the man. But here in Rome I had felt his foot on me for far too long. My policeman! And with him around, I had felt as walled in here in Rome as I had felt in Judea. Well, I was free of him now. I could do what I wanted with my story. The night of his death I took a long walk by myself, feeling young again, and free and light, and soon in my imagination I was walking again in the streets of Jerusalem.

When I got home it was late. Julia was ill in bed with a congestion of the chest, and the servants were asleep. I went to the little room that was full of my books and parchments and took from a secret place in the wall the gem-laden little cedar box I had brought from Judea that held the manuscript. As I looked at the manuscript, I thought, I have a tongue again, a voice to be heard. And I sat down at the table and read.

When I had finished I fell into a trance, seeing it all again, but not thinking at all about it till the scene faded. Then I pondered, and the more I did so, the easier it was to see that the Galilean could not possibly want it to be revealed that Judas was the loving servant who only did his bidding, loving the Galilean to the end. Both in on it — complicity! Nor could the Galilean want it to be revealed that Judas, talking to me, had cleared himself. Oh, what a new light that would put them both in. But it was the truth. And I had it.

But while I sat there pondering I began to feel so restless and physically uncomfortable I had to get up and take some wine. And with the wine warming me, quickening me, yet making me feel the sudden unbearable late-night silence of my own house, and making me listen intently for some little familiar sound, if only that of a night bird, I sat down again. Then with the same trembling wonderment I had felt that night in the Judean hills, I saw myself riding wildly on the road, riding away from the grave with the three stones, after seeing the apparition, the man in the brown coat showing himself to me, and I heard myself crying out, "Why me? Why me?" I was shaken. I got up and drank more wine and was still shaken, for I could still see the Judean hills, the embankment and the road and the figure coming across the moonlit road towards me and Isaiah scrambling after him with his sword raised, and the frightened horses neighing, and then myself riding hard, fleeing from the clearing, then suddenly drawing my horse in, coming to a stop, motionless, moonstruck, whispering, "Why me?"

Though the picture faded quickly from my mind, and though I was here in Rome and it was years later, I was wondering if I now had the answer to that question, "Why me?" Could it be that the Galilean had known that he would need my silence some day? Then the some day was now, and I was a little awed. The Galilean knew he would need my silence, and poor Judas, who could not know, had pleaded for my silence, and could I betray them now?

Exhausted and no longer trusting my thinking, I put

the manuscript away and went to bed, making up my mind to deal with the matter in the morning, in the sunlight, when things look different than they do at night. But in the morning I did not make a decision. Then, as I went about my business I found I could not get the thing out of my mind. It was my use of that word betrayal that was tormenting me. Is the truth ever a betrayal? I wondered. Yes, one man can rat on another. The informer? The eternal rat. All this made me unhappy, and it was hard to do business with anybody, and I took walks by myself, asking such questions as, "Can you lie to tell the truth? Can it be that a lie can serve a greater truth?" Poor Judas, whose heart was broken, because he had told the truth.

At this time, walking by the Tiber and feeling tired, I sat down, watching the flowing river and wondering why it was that so often when my mind was troubled I thought of the ever-changing river. Then again I thought of Judas as if he belonged to a river that had carried him into the great sea. I saw him now as a great human figure. It was true that the poor man talked too much and let the Galilean down, but he knew it. There by the river he began to move me so profoundly that I wanted to clear him at once of the infamy heaped on him. Yet I understood that he did not want to be cleared; it was the last thing in time he wanted; he was where he wanted to be, he was where the Galilean needed him to be in the story — where he had agreed to be.

While I was saying all these things to myself, and believing them, I knew it would break my heart to destroy my story. How could I do it when I knew this story had a wonder and mystery of its own? And yet it was the truth. With all my heart I believed that the truth had a grandeur of its own and could be even more mysterious than the acceptable fables. And I owed something to myself and my own inner domain. I knew I must not betray myself, for if I did, my own inner domain was lost to me; all other betrayals would become easy.

The more I mulled it over, the less certain I was of what I owed to Judas, or what I owed to myself, and I went home. There I remained moody and irritable with the servants and the old woman who looked after my Julia, who still had the fever.

In the middle of the night I heard Julia coughing and got up quickly to get her a drink and smooth her hair. Her forehead to my touch felt quite cool. The fever had broken. Feeling relieved, I sat on the edge of my bed for a few moments, and then after I had put out the lamp and was making my way back to bed again in the dark, it came to me. What I should do with my manuscript came to me, came with a feeling of satisfaction I had to trust.

First I would tell what had happened to me here in Rome after my return from Judea, and add this to the story. Then I would put the manuscript in a sealed jar. But the jar had to be beautiful. I looked around for a tall Greek jar, a blue jar, with carved figures in flight — a jar any man would covet and admire, and I put my manuscript in this jar and sealed the jar and waited to take it to Crete and put it in a secret place in my father's house. I liked thinking of my story being in that beautiful jar.

That the story should not be read now was not important. It would be there, existing, though hidden, waiting to be seen and read. Before this could happen, grass might grow over those three stones on the hillside, and wars pass over them too, and everything molder into dust. Soon even the hill might not be there. But when the time came, as surely it would, if I was right about the grandeur of truth, if the time was right for an end to the unbearable loneliness of Judas in the minds of all men on earth, then the story would be found and read.